GORILLA MOUNTAIN

Book Five in the Green Watch series

by
Anthony Masters
Illustrated by Pauline Hazelwood

Hippo Books
Scholastic Publications Limited
London

255747

Scholastic Publications Ltd,
10 Earlham Street, London WC2H 9RX, UK

Scholastic Inc.,
730 Broadway, New York, NY 10003, USA

Scholastic Canada Ltd,
123 Newkirk Road, Richmond Hill,
Ontario L4C 3G5, Canada

Ashton Scholastic Pty Ltd,
P O Box 579, Gosford, New South Wales,
Australia

Ashton Scholastic Ltd,
Private Bag 1, Penrose, Auckland,
New Zealand

First published in the UK by Scholastic Publications Ltd, 1991

Text copyright © Anthony Masters, 1991
Illustration copyright © Pauline Hazelwood, 1991

ISBN 0 590 76578 7

Typeset by AKM Associates (UK) Ltd, Southall, London
Printed by Cox and Wyman Ltd, Reading, Berks
10 9 8 7 6 5 4 3 2 1

Prologue

Group Two were moving further up the mountain. They didn't want to, for the higher they climbed the colder and wetter it grew, but the poachers were driving them on and they were terrified. Their feeding trail had narrowed to a single track and they had flattened plants and bushes around it. Cloud thickened on the mountainside, and slivers of mist made the gorillas look insubstantial to each other as they fed on the giant lobelia, grunting quietly as they broke open the stems with their strong fingers and scraped out the pulp.

They were jumpy – all of them – looking down the trail and up at the twin volcanoes above them. The slightest movement in the undergrowth would cause the large male silverback to bound aggressively

1

forward, leaving the other six a chattering, shuddering heap of dark hair. When standing, he was enormous – nearly 170 centimetres high, with a huge narrow head and short muscular arms. But now he was feeding with the others, his favourite mate beside him. Her children were beginning to play among the gnarled hagenia trees whose damp, sinuous branches were covered in vines, ferns and mosses. His other mate, a smaller female, was quietly feeding her baby.

After a while the three children bounded through the trees, play-fighting with each other or their parents. Occasionally the silverback would capture one of them, hugging the child to him, rocking it to and fro, gently pressing and caressing it. Then the group slept, either in the fork of a tree or on the ground. But they slept lightly, snatching their rest rather than enjoying it, while the mist began to build up around them. It was as if they were being driven into uneasy exile by their enemies below. Now there was nowhere they could take their rest – or make their journeys – without feeling hunted.

An hour later the group rose and, led by the silverback, slowly began to move further up the damp mountainside. In a single line they climbed warily on until a female child left the trail to eat a particularly succulent-looking vernonia flower. It lay on another well-worn path. Too late, the silverback turned to bellow a warning. With a terrible scream the gorilla-child was lifted off the ground by her leg and hung there crying and chattering, her face screwed up in agony. She had walked into a snare.

2

The vicious wire loop was attached to a bamboo pole which had been bent over and secured. When the child's foot caught in the wire loop, the pole had jerked free and lifted her violently off the ground. Now she hung there, biting and pulling at the pole while the rest of the group gathered round, filled with her reflected pain. Eventually, after frantic, agonising activity, she freed herself and fell to the ground with a horrendous thud. Her mother hurried to her, licking and caressing her leg. But her daughter had not survived the trap uninjured. The wire loop had bitten deeply into her leg, and however hard they tried, there was nothing they could do to remove it. The wound was already oozing crimson blood. The silverback roared and beat his chest with cupped hands. The traps had been sprung on so many of his kind recently and he knew instinctively that the wound with the wire still in it would soon become septic and, slowly and painfully, she would die.

He beat his chest again in a terrible frustration, for he knew that there was nothing, absolutely nothing, that he could do to save her – or any of them. Constant vigilance was not enough. Soon they would all die.

Chapter One

Green Watch sat at the round table in the converted windmill that was the Howards' home on the Romney Marsh, and where they lived between projects. It was a warm night and the scent of grass and mint came in from the herb garden by the stream.

To Seb Howard's right sat his wife Anne, and then Flower and Brian, his children, and their cousin Tim. From the start, Green Watch had deliberately remained small – just a family affair. Tim was proud to be part of the family. His dad had just come out of prison and had gone on a re-training scheme as a farm manager. Tim and Mum had been helping and supporting Dad as much as possible, but now both his parents had insisted that he should stay with his cousins for a few days and go to the Green Watch meeting. Seb had phoned and told them an exciting trip was in the offing and they wanted him to take advantage of it. His dad had even said that Green Watch had "made a person of him", and although Tim wasn't quite sure what that meant, it indicated that his dad was pleased and didn't seem to be in the least jealous of the people his son had spent so much time with while he was in prison.

Now as they sat round the table no one knew what Seb and Anne were going to say, but they quickly picked up an atmosphere of tension.

"Hear him out," said Anne. "Just hear him out."

This is going to be bad news, thought Tim suddenly. They all knew something was up, for Flower and Brian had already told him that both Seb and Anne had been anxious for weeks now.

Seb began hesitantly – so hesitantly that they all stared at him in surprise.

"You may not like this, but bear with me. I know I should have told you earlier, but I've been trying to find ways round the problem – and failing."

He's tired, thought Tim, and apprehensive. Seb's normally well-tanned face was grey with fatigue and there were bags under his eyes. Anne looked concerned and kept darting him worried glances.

"Anne and I have to go away for a few months."

"Where?" asked Flower anxiously, staring at him in bewilderment. Brian said nothing but Tim felt a trembling sensation in his fingertips.

"The South Pole," he replied flatly.

"How long?" asked Brian. There was considerable agitation in his voice.

"Six months. Auntie Grace will be taking over here."

"Yuck!" said Flower. "She's awful."

Tim saw that there were tears in her eyes and Brian was looking away.

Seb continued quickly, "We've been asked to join an Antarctic survey to monitor the hole in the ozone layer. We'll be part of a group of scientists and conservationists measuring its rate of growth and—" He broke off. "Oh, well – I can tell you the rest later."

"Why can't we come?" Tim felt that he was speaking for them all.

"School," said Seb. "You'd be missing rather a lot of it."

"Does that matter?" asked Flower, and Tim could see she was struggling to keep back the tears.

"I think so."

"You've always taken us before," said Brian. "Why not this time?"

"We don't have any money left," Anne said gently. So far she had been very careful to say nothing. Seb's first wife had left him when the children were quite young, and as Anne had only recently married him she felt she had to tread cautiously. She had built up a good relationship with Flower and Brian, but Tim knew she was wondering whether this announcement was going to wreck all they had worked for.

"She's right." Seb sounded reluctant to talk about it. "We haven't a bean left and couldn't afford to take you with us for such a long time. But if we join the survey we'll be bringing in a double income, as well as being able to lecture and write about it when we come home."

"OK," said Brian angrily. "So it's all wrapped up." His voice shook.

"No it isn't," replied Anne suddenly, and Seb turned to her angrily.

"What's that?"

"This isn't emotional blackmail," she said, "but there is an alternative."

This time it was Seb's turn to say, "No, Anne. No chance."

"There is," she said grimly.

"We discussed it and—"

"We're wrong to decide everything ourselves. Everyone in Green Watch should know the facts and help us reach a decision."

"Anne—"

"Will you two get on with it?" snapped Flower, wiping away her tears.

"Anne could get a job as a teacher and I could get some kind of university post," said Seb.

Flower looked horrified and Brian sighed. "It just isn't you."

"Then there's no way out," said Anne. "But don't think we didn't offer the idea seriously. Isn't that right, Seb?"

He nodded reluctantly. "If you really pushed us, we'd do the teaching."

"We're not pushing you," said Flower. "Are we, Brian? Tim?"

They chorused that they weren't, but all three felt hollow inside.

"There's something else." Seb spoke abruptly. "I don't know if you'll think it's a sop, but a magazine rang up to see if you three would like to do some reporting on a group of gorillas. They'd pay the fare and expenses as well as some kind of fee."

"Gorillas?" repeated Brian. "Why us? Where?"

"Africa," said Anne. "With an old friend of mine, Alison Best. She's rather special; she used to be a vet in Suffolk but she and her husband John – he's a vet too – got interested in the persecution of some groups of gorillas in the Virunga mountains. It's quite a small national park, about fifty kilometres long and only ten to twenty-five wide, and it's the very last stronghold of the mountain gorilla. The mountains are really six extinct volcanoes and the area's shared by Rwanda, Zaire and Uganda." She paused, looking round at the three younger members of Green Watch, wondering how they were taking it all. "Alison and John have been there for about ten years now, and I went out a couple of years ago – well before I met you all. They've set up a base in this incredibly beautiful spot; I'll never ever forget it. It's about 3,000 metres up in the saddle between two of the extinct volcanoes. It's the most mystical place I've ever been to: grassy glades divided by a stream so clear that you can see even the tiniest pebble at the bottom, and surrounded by lots of yellow hypericum flower trees covered with pale green lichen. Incredible. I can show you some photos later. Alison and John have built a couple of huts out of corrugated iron hung with grass matting; it's really cold at night there." She paused again but now Flower, Brian and Tim were listening with rapt attention. "The gorillas have been driven up into the hagenia forest – that's huge old trees draped with moss and lichen and ferns and vines. It's very cold and damp in the forest."

"Driven there by who?" asked Tim.

"Poachers. They're usually after bushbuck and small antelopes, but gorillas easily fall into the traps and snares they set up, and although they can sometimes get out of the traps they can't get rid of the wire that cuts into their wrists and ankles – and this becomes infected."

"So they die," said Flower.

"Slowly and painfully," replied Seb. "Anne's seen one, haven't you?"

She nodded. "Anyway, John and Alison have been fighting a campaign against the poachers. There was someone else in the area before them – an American woman called Dian Fossey who lived with the gorillas and became accepted by them. She fought against the poachers but was eventually murdered, probably by one of them."

"Will they go that far against John and Alison?" asked Flower.

Anne shrugged. "I hope they don't. The

9

anti-poaching patrols have been stepped up by the park rangers and so on, but with the Rwanda population growing so quickly and a shortage of land for families to grow food, some people are bound to hunt for meat in the forest, and sell skins to buy food, and the poor old gorillas just get caught in the traps and are being decimated."

"I've never done any writing for a magazine before," said Brian abruptly.

Despite their genuine interest in the gorillas, Tim could see that Flower and Brian were still very upset about the situation.

"You'll be fine." Seb sounded briskly confident. "All you have to do is observe and take notes. The Bests have got brilliant photographs they'll let you have – and one of the desk editors from the magazine will help you write the article when you get back."

"OK," said Flower. "If it'll help with the money."

"The fee will be divided amongst the three of you," began Seb, but Flower shook her head.

"No chance. It goes into the family pool or we don't take it." She turned to the others for confirmation and they nodded.

"You're brilliant!" said Anne, but Flower quickly changed the subject.

"Tell us more about the Bests," she said. Tim saw that there were still tears in her eyes and he felt a great sadness himself. The Howards were such a close family.

"John and Alison have done what Dian Fossey did;

they've been accepted by a gorilla group – and what I saw was one of the most marvellous experiences of my life," said Anne enthusiastically.

"Were *you* accepted, Anne?" asked Flower.

"I wasn't there long enough – just a few days. But if you three went there for a few weeks—"

"Do they want us?" asked Tim anxiously.

"Yes." Seb was very confident. "We spoke to them on the phone yesterday. Alison is going to be in the capital, Kigali, picking up supplies, so she could meet you at the airport."

"When?" Brian looked up curiously.

"Friday." Seb was grinning.

"It's Tuesday today," he said gloomily. "What about tickets?"

"The magazine will fix them."

"Is it dangerous out there?" asked Tim.

"No," replied Seb. "They take tourists out to see the gorillas. You just have to do what Alison and John tell you."

"And they *really* want us?" asked Flower suspiciously.

"Guaranteed," said Anne crisply. "They're old friends – good people. They want to share their experiences – they've always wanted to. Besides, your reputation precedes you."

"Well?" asked Seb. "So what's the answer?"

There was a long silence. Then Flower looked at the others. "I want to go," she said.

"So do I." Brian smiled for the first time and looked at Tim. "What about you?"

"I'm on. But Mum—"

Seb gave him an appraising glance. "You know how much we all value you, Tim, and the brilliant things you've done for Green Watch. I'll speak to your mum and dad – I'm sure they'll agree."

"Thanks, Seb." Tim was delighted.

Flower reached out for her father's hand. "We're going to miss you. Both of you," she added, and Brian nodded.

"We don't want to split up like this." Seb was adamant.

"We'll just have to pray the time passes quickly," said Anne. There was a break in her voice now and she looked away.

"We'll have to get through this," replied Brian. "All of us. But once this cash crisis is over—"

"We'll be together again." Seb's voice had a quiet certainty.

Chapter Two

The heat met them with considerable force directly they stepped out on the tarmac. But there was something else – a particular smell which they couldn't define.

"It's Africa," said Flower and both boys knew exactly what she meant.

Once they had checked out of the one-storied airport building they stood blinking in the sunlight which was still very bright, although it was late in the afternoon, feeling lost and peculiar. Even Tim, often absorbed in his own home difficulties, picked up a little of what the Howards were feeling. Here they were, thousands of kilometres away from home in an alien country, while Seb and Anne flew to the South Pole. When they got home there would only be

Auntie Grace at the windmill, and the magazine editor's expectations. The further irony was that now they had arrived in Rwanda there was no one to greet them – only a dusty road, some battered advertising hoardings and a couple of beat-up taxis whose drivers eyed them curiously.

Then, with a squeal of brakes, an open land-rover covered in dust and mud screeched to a halt. Behind the wheel was a tall bronzed woman with dark hair and dark glasses. Beside her sat an elderly black man with silvery hair.

"Green Watch?"

"That's us," said Brian hesitantly.

"I'm Alison – this is Dan." Her voice was deep, casual, yet had a certain authority to it. "Get aboard – we've got a long way to go."

They struggled with their baggage, and if any of them had thought that Dan might help them, they were wrong. He nodded at them with a quiet dignity and Tim felt his presence was very strong.

"Dan's one of the national park guides," Alison said suddenly. "There isn't anything he doesn't know about gorillas."

Dan stared gently ahead. There was something mysterious about him, as if part of his mind was somewhere else.

But Alison was the opposite, and she was all too interested in them. One by one she cross-examined them about themselves and Green Watch, and it was only when they had travelled several kilometres that she seemed to be satisfied.

"Where are we going?" asked Flower.

"We're going to the Virunga; it's about four hours by car from here. Hope you're not going to be too tired."

"We'll be fine," said Brian. "Won't we, Tim?" He nudged him rather sharply because Tim was dozing off already; Brian didn't want the formidable Alison to think they were wimps. Tim jerked awake, aware of Alison's steely hands on the steering wheel. It was difficult to imagine that she had once practised as a vet somewhere in England. Aware of their scrutiny she laughed, and the atmosphere changed immediately.

"What do you lot think I am – the white hunter type?"

Dan laughed too, a soft, melodious loving sound that made them feel even better. These people are human after all, thought Tim.

"From the way you three look, it seems you're expecting me to test you out; make you paddle over a waterfall in a dug-out canoe or wrestle a crocodile."

Dan laughed again while Flower and Brian joined in awkwardly. It's more or less what I was beginning to think you *would* make us do, thought Tim uneasily.

"We don't expect – want – that sort of rubbish, but you do have to be brave. For instance, one thing you must never do is to run away from a charging gorilla."

"No?" asked Brian. "That might be my first idea."

"Let it be your last," said Alison. "You have to stand your ground."

"And don't make contact with the eyes," put in Dan, speaking at last. "It represents a challenge."

"Do you ever get near enough?" asked Tim. "To make contact with the eyes, I mean?"

15

"Oh yes," said Alison. "You'll get near enough, but don't let me wind you up about it. The gorilla group you're going to spend time with is very loving, and it's really moving to be with them." She paused. "It's become my life – and Dan and John's too."

She talked on in little bursts over the next two hours, while the scenery changed from the great flat plain they were traversing to scrubbier bush and later to the rising mass of the Virunga mountains. It was early evening and dark shadows were lengthening on the road that was getting more rutted and pot-holed by the minute. Then Alison swung the land-rover on to a narrower, even rougher road, and the trees seemed to close over their heads.

"Have you given the gorillas names?" asked Flower tentatively, wondering if she was sounding silly or sentimental or both. Maybe they just had numbers like some herds of cows did.

"Oh yes," Alison replied, smiling. "We had to identify them somehow, so John and I gave them the names of some of our aunts and uncles. There's Albert – he's the leader – and he's got two wives, Helena and Sylvia. Sylvia has a baby, Tommy – she had two actually but one seems to have disappeared – and Helena has three children, Sampson, Juniper and Jocasta." Suddenly she brought the vehicle to a stop and raised a finger to her lips. "Listen," she said.

Alison turned off the engine and, dutifully at first, they listened.

"This is Africa," she whispered. "Sit very still; let it come into you."

They did as she told them, and gradually it all began to happen. The land-rover had stopped in the middle of a small clearing and suddenly they felt immersed in an unseen world of movement and sound that came from the bush around them. Clickings, stirrings, shufflings, sudden darting movements were mixed with whirring, hooting, guttural calling and occasional chattering. It was incredible; they were on the surface of a wild inner world of life that was working at a feverish pace. A moth flew past them, huge and soft and white with blue markings. It cruised around them for a minute or so, coming very close as they sat hardly daring to breathe. The moth was like a messenger from the bush come to view them and report back to the mystical scurrying inside.

"That's what I've fallen in love with," said Alison. "The unseen, unspoilt life. The place is teeming with it – hundreds of different forms." She switched on the engine and its roar seemed like a tropical storm. Somewhere above the sound, the high chattering increased indignantly and the moth darted back into the velvety darkness with a last flash of white silky light.

They drove for another hour, with the road getting worse until the land-rover was rocking crazily all the time. Yet none of the three felt sick, and despite the unpredictability of the rocking it began to create an almost soothing pattern in Tim's mind. He noticed that Dan was driving now – he must have dropped off and not noticed the changeover – and that Alison was sitting bolt upright with her eyes closed. He looked at the others; they were all dropping off in the warm scented night and, at last, Tim felt that he was permitted to sleep. He slowly nodded off, feeling relaxed and easy, with all the tension of the flight and the awkward first meeting draining out of him.

Tim dreamed of his dad and the day they had met him at the gates of the prison. At the time he had looked much smaller than Tim had imagined he would, and in the dream he was tiny, with a minute battered suitcase and a trailing scarf against the wintery weather. Tim picked him up under his arm and, walking with his mother like two great giants, took him down to a café for a cup of tea. But in the café their rôles were reversed and his father became huge while he and Mum shrank to the size of tiny children, their legs swinging free of the ground as they sat on enormous chairs, their chins just coming up to table height, trying to tackle the giant cups while his father burst into a song about the Yeomen of England. Then he woke to an enormous bump and silence. He was cold, and when he looked up at the sky he could see clouds racing over the face of a large white moon and the peaks of what looked like mountains but were probably the ancient volcanoes of Virunga.

A tree was lying across the narrow road, and Alison had jumped down to look at it while Dan stood on the land-rover's running board. He had something in his hand, which Tim slowly realised was a rifle, and he was covering Alison, staring down its sights. Tim shivered; they must be climbing into the mountains now, for it was really quite cold. He glanced across at Flower, who was looking composed, as she often did, and at Brian, who was looking vague, as *he* often did, but there was an underlying uneasiness to both of them. Why was the tree across the path? Tim wondered. Had there been a gale or something? He didn't like to ask; everyone was so silent and Alison seemed tense as she stood by the fallen tree, her eyes darting round the glade.

"Can we shift it?" she said to Dan.

He nodded.

"I don't like it." She scanned the glade again. Everything seemed very still, and there wasn't nearly as much movement and sound in the undergrowth. To Tim, it seemed that everything was on a kind of brink – poised, waiting. But waiting for what?

"OK." Alison stood looking up at them, hands on hips. "Looks like one of life's little mysteries." She smiled, her tanned face dark in the night and her teeth gleaming white. They all felt better and she said, "It won't take long to get it out of the way."

"How did it fall?" asked Brian, but Alison either didn't hear or chose to ignore him as she began to give instructions to Dan about backing up the land-rover and getting out some rope.

In minutes, Dan had the rope around the tree and the vehicle hitched up to it.

"Stay where you are," she told them, suddenly making them feel useless. Then, as if realising how much they wanted to help, she said gently, "You won't be spectators when we get up to base; you're going to be really involved."

Dan turned the land-rover in a wide arc through the undergrowth so that the tree began to swing round at an angle. He was just finishing the manoeuvre when Flower shouted above the roar of the engine.

"Who's that?"

Dan switched off the ignition immediately and the awful stillness resumed. He looked enquiringly at Flower and Alison snapped,

"What's up?" Her voice was tight and strained.

"I saw someone." Flower stuttered as she spoke and her eyes were wild and searching. Brian put his arm round her.

"Probably just a trick of the—"

"I *saw* someone," she said shortly, shrugging free.

"Where?" asked Alison, more calmly.

"There – I *know* I saw someone," she half sobbed out of a mixture of fear and exhaustion.

Dan turned his calm face round to her and touched her hand. "Don't worry – I know you saw someone." He stood up in the land-rover and took out his rifle again, sweeping the bush, his eyes, like Alison's intent on the smallest movement.

Then he sat down again, started the engine and

slowly the tree began to swing out of the road. A small animal leapt out of the way – it was impossible for Tim to see what it was – and there was a cracking sound, as if a large number of sharp twigs were being snapped. When Tim looked at Dan again, he was crouched forward in a very odd position over the wheel, as if he was trying to reach down for something. Then Brian yelled.

"Alison – Alison!"

She was lying half over the tree which was still moving, because, as Tim suddenly realised, so was the land-rover. Gradually it swung into an immense tree and stopped, it's engine stalling.

"They've been shot," said Brian, the shock making him sound almost matter-of-fact.

"What?" Flower stared at Dan unbelievingly. There was a dark patch on his white T-shirt. "What are you on about?"

"He's been shot. Don't touch him."

"Alison!" Grabbing a torch, Flower leapt out of the land-rover and ran towards her. She was still lying over the tree, and there was a spreading stain on her bush shirt just above the elbow.

"Go away," Alison said.

"I've got to help you."

"Run – for God's sake – run! All of you."

"There're people coming," said Brian from the land-rover. Tim bent over Dan, trying to communicate with him, but although his lips moved no words

21

came. The sound of crashing undergrowth was on top of them now, and as Flower looked towards the ragged shapes, Alison repeated her instruction.

"I *said* run," she muttered, attempting to pull herself up and then falling back over the foliage. "Please run. Get the others moving. You must!"

But it was too late. The men were walking across the glade towards her, some peeling off to snatch Dan's rifle roughly out of his hand. There were about half a dozen of them, and all of them held guns.

"He's dead!" snapped Tim.

"He's breathing," replied Brian with a quiet authority.

Tim thought of the windmill and the round table and the unruffled quiet of the British countryside. It was great planning, not so good carrying the plans out. If only Seb and Anne had come with them instead of deserting the rest of Green Watch for the South Pole. He felt like closing his eyes and keeping them closed until the men had gone. But they didn't show any signs of moving away. They were all quite young, and simply stood and stared. Eventually one of them attempted to pull Dan away from the wheel, but he slumped back with a groan.

"Leave her!" yelled Flower suddenly. The other group had picked up Alison and were trying to stand her on her feet, but she kept falling forwards like a bobbing doll that Tim had had when he was a baby. The memory returned to him with a horrible sickening feeling. He had been numb before, but now he felt a creeping terror. They were trying to take Alison away and were at last succeeding; with one man on each side they were half carrying, half dragging her towards the bush. Tim and Brian watched helplessly, but Flower sprang forward and tried to stop them. One of them pushed her away and she fell heavily on her back. Brian and Tim were about to run to her rescue when another member of the group aimed his rifle at them and snapped, "Don't move!"

Alison looked up at the sound and said in a voice drained of strength, "Poachers. Get away. They're poachers." Her head slumped forward and she seemed to lapse into unconsciousness. But still they dragged her away and, seconds later, she was swallowed up in the bush.

Chapter Three

For a moment, Tim thought he was going to be shot. He stared transfixed as the man jerked the rifle barrel at him. Then he realised he was being told to get out of the land-rover, and so was Brian. They scrambled off the vehicle and joined Flower, who was sitting up and beginning to yell at the two men left beside her.

"Bring her back!"

They stared down at her inscrutably.

"Go on – bring her back!"

Still no response.

"Bring her *back*!"

"She OK," one of them said finally.

"She's not!" yelled Flower.

By now they were pulling Dan roughly out of the

land-rover and dumping him in the clearing. He groaned and rolled over on his front.

"He's hurt – he's in agony," said Tim. "You've got to help him."

"He'll be fine," said one of the men quietly as he climbed in behind the wheel of the land-rover. Slowly, almost lethargically, the others strolled over and got in. Then they drove off through the under-growth in the direction the other men and Alison had taken, and Tim could see the beginnings of a kind of path in the headlights. They were gone.

Tim stared in disbelief. This just *couldn't* have happened. They were on their own with a badly wounded man, and Alison had just been shot and kid-napped. They had no idea of where they were or where they were going. He gulped back the panic and said,

"We'd better take a look at Dan – see if we can help him at all."

The others stared at him, dazed, and then Flower agreed, "Of course we should."

Feeling better at having something to do, they went over to Dan and knelt down beside him. He seemed to be just conscious and his breathing was deep but regular.

"Dan—" They all had First Aid certificates but Brian was the Green Watch member who was best at administering it. "Dan," he repeated.

There was an answering mumble but it wasn't distinguishable.

"Dan," Brian repeated, "I'm going to cut away your shirt and take a look at the wound. Is that OK?"

Again the mumble, which he took as assent. Brian brought out his pocket knife and hacked away at the material, but the knife was blunt which made cutting difficult. Eventually he had done all he could and a large, ragged hole exposed a nasty looking wound. It was wide and looked as if the bullet had gone in at an angle.

"I think it's still in there," said Brian. "Just below the shoulder." He tried to lift Dan but he couldn't, and it was only with the help of the others that he eventually managed to move him so that he could see his shoulder better. There was no mark on the other side. "It hasn't come out," said Brian gloomily.

"Then what are we going to do?" asked Flower. She was on her knees, holding the torch and staring hopelessly at Dan.

Brian and Tim exchanged glances. This was awful. Throughout their last four adventures, Flower had never seemed to be at such a loss. She was always so versatile and full of initiative. Tim looked around him and shivered. He knew how she felt; this must be the most hostile environment they had ever been in. The darkness was a kind of heavy velvet and now they were quiet the scufflings and unidentifiable noises were returning. He was also sure that he could see tiny darts of light in the undergrowth. Were they sharp eyes, watching them? It was all elemental, alien, out there, and there was nothing, nobody, that would or could help them.

"We'll have to get to John – to the base. It can't be far."

"But which way?" she asked wildly, looking round. "We haven't got anything – not even a compass."

"Dan will know," said Brian solidly.

"He's unconscious," she replied.

"He'll come round."

"Are you proposing we carry him?" Her voice was shrill, uncontrolled. Then she made a visible effort, struggling to remain calm and rational. "Sorry, of course he'll know the way. And maybe he'll be able to walk. Slowly, I mean."

Tim looked down at Dan doubtfully and exchanged another covert look with Brian. Flower had lost all sense of balance; she was darting from one extreme to the other. Dan hadn't even returned to consciousness yet, and as for walking – but they both knew they had to try. Brian slapped Dan's cheeks gently – and then harder.

"Dan, you've got to wake up. Please."

One eye flickered open and then closed again.

"Wake *up*, Dan. We need your help."

"What?" The eyes were open now but kept flickering alarmingly. "What do you want?" His voice was a threat.

"Your help," said Flower. She was her old self now and she sounded very calm. "We need your help."

"Help?" His eyes were flickering faster.

"Alison. They shot her and took her away."

His eyes were steadier now and they could see he

27

was making a fantastic effort to concentrate. At the same time, his face was twisted with pain.

"Shot?"

"I don't think – it was in the arm. She said they were poachers." Brian's words poured out in a torrent and he repeated them more slowly.

Dan nodded. "They've been waiting for her."

"What are they going to do?" asked Tim.

"I don't know." He winced again in pain. "They're – you can't tell."

"You've got a bullet in the shoulder." Brian spoke with surprising authority. "And it's still there."

Dan grimaced. "You're talking straight."

"I've got to."

Dan closed his eyes but they could see he was only resting. When he opened them again, he said, "Walking, we're about four – five – hours from base. Maybe more – if I could walk," he added.

Four or five hours? They looked at one another in horror. It was nearly eight o'clock already – John would begin to worry about them soon.

"Can you try?"

"I can try." He began to pull himself to his feet but collapsed, clasping his shoulder, tears in his eyes.

"Have we got a first aid kit?" asked Flower.

Dan shook his head. "In the land-rover."

Tim groaned.

"Everything in the land-rover," muttered Dan.

"Including water?" Tim suddenly asked.

He nodded again, but then said, "We can find water. First – fix poultice. Slap it on wound. Be numbing."

28

"How do we do that?" asked Brian.

"First you find big broad leaves with yellow outside and then get little red plant. Bring them to me – quick as you can. It's throbbing bad now."

Dan lay back on the ground and closed his eyes. It's like a treasure hunt, thought Tim, except that we haven't got a chance of finding anything. He and Brian searched and Flower flashed the torch. Tim wondered how long they would have to go on before they admitted defeat. It was an impossible job with only one torch – just as impossible as the thought of Dan ever being able to put one foot in front of the other.

"Blimey!" said Brian, who was a few metres away from him, scouring the undergrowth.

"What's up?"

"There's dozens of 'em."

Tim joined him and it was true enough; in a patch of moonlight little red plants sprouted all over the place.

"Here it is!" Flower's voice boomed out from the other side of the glade and something near them scampered away with sharp little grunts. "Big broad leaves with a yellow outside."

They quickly gathered some together and hurried back to the centre of the clearing with armfuls of the two different types of plant.

"They're all over the place," said Flower.

Tim immediately cheered up. It was like a sign of hope. If healing flowers grew in such abundance, then maybe Dan might make it after all. But something in the dark part of his mind told him that was very unlikely.

They rubbed the leaves together to Dan's instructions until they had the right kind of moist, compressed mass.

"Put it on the wound," he said at last.

Brian took the mess and paused.

"Go on."

"Won't it hurt?"

"Of course. Then it will stop hurting."

Still Brian hesitated.

"Go on," Dan insisted. "Press it on."

Hurriedly, Brian pressed it gently on to the wound. Dan squirmed; there was no doubt that it was really hurting him. Then he relaxed with a sigh.

"Do you know the way?" asked Flower. "The way to the base?"

"Of course."

"Will the poachers come back?"

"Not now they have her."

"What will they do?" asked Tim forlornly.

"I don't know. Ransom, maybe. Or – worse."

No one spoke. Suddenly none of them wanted to ask any more questions.

Dan staggered to his feet. "It feels better." He pulled a knife with a long, sharp blade from his belt. "Cut me a walking stick," he said to Flower. "Something strong."

While she hacked at a very solid-looking tree,

Brian and Tim conferred, just out of earshot of Dan, who was taking hesitant little steps up and down the clearing.

"You hungry?" asked Tim.

"Starving."

"Shall we ask him if there's anything to eat out here?"

"Probably only fresh lion," replied Brian gloomily.

"Shall I ask him?" Tim was impatient, for the hunger was really gnawing at him now.

"Let's get moving first," was the grim reply.

Meanwhile Flower returned with the knife and a stout stick. She gave both to Dan, who leant his weight on the branch and pronounced himself satisfied. But Tim could see sweat standing out on his brow and the night was quite chilly.

"You OK?" he asked Dan.

"Well – only got me a bullet in the shoulder."

Tim felt foolish but Dan grinned. "I'll survive. That's what they say, isn't it?"

"I don't know," said Brian dolefully. "I suppose some do."

They began to walk slowly uphill, following Dan who walked steadily but awkwardly. How long can he keep it up? Tim wondered. But the pace suited him and gradually, as they climbed, the foliage became spooky with huge, gnarled trees standing either side of the track rather like old men hung with cobwebs. They – and the track – seemed endless, and somehow it was as if they were marking time rather than walking.

Pangs of hunger made Tim's stomach feel as if there was something rattling about painfully in a huge empty space, and he was sure the others felt the same. But still they plodded on, following the slow-moving Dan who never once paused to speak or to look back at them.

Suddenly he did stop and they all practically cannoned into him.

"Look," he said.

The path had risen sharply here, and through the tracery of vine and lichen they could see both valley and mountains etched in clear moonlight. It was an amazing sight, with hard-edged trees, white rock, lush jungle and bare, silver-glinting lower peaks. There was a scattering of huts to one side but no other sign of habitation. All around them the chattering and scuffling was rarely silent. Tim looked up; the moon was full and white and beautiful, riding high in a sky full of swollen scudding clouds as a sharp wind picked up and rustled its way through the foliage.

Glancing at Dan, Tim could see that his face was now completely bathed in sweat and, worse still, he was shaking all over. Was this sudden, or had he been plodding on in this state for the last hour?

"How long is it to go?" asked Flower, pulling up the collar of her shirt.

"Another three hours. At least."

"You're shaking."

"Got a fever."

"Are you going to make it?" asked Tim, realising to his shame that he was more concerned for his own fate than Dan's. Why couldn't he be less selfish in this crisis?

"Course I'm going to make it." He looked cross at what he obviously felt was patronage.

"Sorry."

"That's all right. You have to remember something."

"What's that?" asked Tim contritely.

"I live here. I'm African."

How did that make any difference to a gun wound? Tim wondered. He looked around at the rustling undergrowth. Where were the poachers now? Far away or lurking nearby, maybe planning to kill them? And what about Alison? Was she alive or dead? The questions buzzed in his mind like a swarm of mosquitoes.

"So." Dan leant up against a tree and something flew out of it angrily. Was it some kind of bat? It zoomed over their heads like a huge flying mouse with an expression of demonic fury on its face. The appearance disturbed them even more. Gradually exhaustion was draining hope and spirit out of all three members of Green Watch.

"Are you hungry?"

"Hungry?" Flower sat down suddenly. "I've been dreaming about baked beans."

"I've been thinking about loads of chips," said Brian. "And a bucket of coke – and that's not coal."

Dan grinned, despite his fever. "Coca Cola has even penetrated the Virunga mountains." He paused while Brian tried to work out whether he had been patronising or not. But his hunger was too pressing. Was Dan going to offer them something to eat? If so, where from?

"And you – you're Tim, aren't you?"

"That's right. I've been thinking about pints of milk shakes and pasta with a really rich tomato sauce."

Dan nodded his head. "I'm afraid I can't offer you that, but you could try these."

"What are they?" asked Brian rather suspiciously.

"It's a fruit."

He pulled a melon-like fruit off the tree and passed it to Flower. "Try it," he said. "Break it in half." The boys moved to the tree quickly and raided it, splitting the fruit in half as quickly as they could and stuffing it into their mouths. It was refreshing but not very substantial. However, it was better than nothing. Tim ate a great deal and still felt hungry but he couldn't face any more. Glancing at Flower and Brian he knew they were thinking the same. Then he looked at Dan; he was still leaning against the tree, but he was shivering now and his eyes were closed.

"Dan."

"Mm."

"*Can* you go on?" Tim's voice was urgent.

Dan jerked awake. "Yeah."

"You sure?"

"Just follow," he grunted.

He started to move on again, but he was stumbling now and Flower tried to stop him. "*You* have something to eat – you must!" she said in concern. But Dan gently pushed her away.

Tim glanced at the others anxiously. Just how long was Dan going to last?

Chapter Four

They stumbled on for at least another hour and Tim felt his ankles and thighs becoming like lead weights. The ground continued to rise steeply and the air seemed to get thinner and colder. Then, quite suddenly, Dan stopped, started again – and keeled over, lying flat on his face. As they gathered round him, Brian said, "Look, the blood's oozing out of that wound again."

"What can we do?" asked Flower.

"Put another poultice on." He bent over Dan and gently raised his head.

"I'll get some leaves."

"Mm."

"Will that help?"

"Alison – Group Two – are they OK?"

Tim gasped. Dan wasn't going anywhere. The fever really had him in its grip now, and he was obviously hallucinating, or at best just rambling.

"It's not Alison – it's Brian. Green Watch."

"Group Two are in trouble."

"It's me, Flower. Alison was kidnapped." She tried desperately to get through to him but there was no recognition whatsoever.

"What are we going to do?" asked Brian hopelessly, trying not to panic.

Tim knelt down by Dan. "How far is it?" But he made no reply and Tim shook his good shoulder as hard as he dared. "Dan, you *must* help us."

He groaned and his eyes flickered open.

"How long – how long to the base?"

"Two hours – fast walking."

"We can help you. Carry you." The suggestion was ludicrous; he was far too heavy even for all three of them.

"Bivouac," he whispered.

"What?"

"Make bivouac." His eyes closed again.

"Make a camp," said Flower. "A shelter – leave him in it and go for help."

"What about the poachers?" wailed Tim.

"That's a chance we've got to take," she snapped. "We can't carry him. We'll go as fast as we can and bring back help. Maybe we could hide him."

"What about animals?" asked Brian.

"I don't know." She seemed close to tears now – a

despair wrought of exhaustion and fear. "We'll just have to take the risk. But we need directions." Flower bent over Dan. "We're going to hide you in a bivouac and bring back help as quickly as we can. But you've got to tell us where we should go. If we get lost that'll be it."

He didn't reply and his eyes remained closed.

"Dan!"

Still no reply.

"For God's sake, Dan!"

One eye flickered blearily open and she shook at his good shoulder.

"Dan – we're going to hide you in a bivouac and go to the base and get help. But we must know where to go."

He nodded but still didn't speak, and seemed to be slipping back into unconsciousness. Then he made a tremendous effort and whispered, "Keep on up – just keep going. You'll come – base. Get John."

Tim simply hoped against hope that Dan was right and his mind hadn't been clouded by the fever.

"OK," said Flower. "Let's make the bivouac."

They spent about half an hour building an effective shelter amongst the trees, thatching it with canes and some big flat leaves that grew nearby. When they had finished they gently and cautiously half pulled and half carried Dan into it. Then they began to bind and weave the nearby undergrowth around the bivouac to camouflage it as much as possible.

"Is he going to be OK?" asked Brian, looking worried.

Flower shrugged. "It's the best we can do. Let's get going. The quicker we get there, the greater his chances are going to be."

The last haul up to the base was definitely the worst part of an already appalling journey. Time after time, Tim felt that he just couldn't go on – that the hard surface under his trainers would eventually make his feet so sore that he just wouldn't be able to put one foot in front of the other. But somehow he did; painfully, doggedly, he staggered on, his pace slow but persistent. He knew the others were feeling the same; every so often he heard a muttered prayer or a little gasp of hopelessness. But still they plodded on until, after the first hour, Flower called a halt. Despite his exhaustion. Tim smiled, noticing that Flower had become their leader. It was her spirit, he supposed, that made her hang on grimly and in the end successfully. She had more gritty determination than he or Brian but she also had something else. Maybe it was a kind of vision, he thought, that made her able to see ahead more clearly. Not just straight ahead up the track, but on into the future so that for her the base was coming closer and closer, whereas he felt that it remained the same distance away.

By now it was eleven-thirty and at least they were noticeably further up the mountains. All three sank down, staring mesmerised at the valley below them, with its moonlit contours and dark clusters of trees.

Only the rock shone up at them, eerily white and luminous. Then something moved in the undergrowth behind them. It was more than the scamperings and scurryings they had become used to; it sounded like a footfall and then there were several of them. Suddenly they stopped. Waiting.

"Don't move," said Flower. "Just keep still."

"What is it?" Tim blurted out.

"How do I know?"

"Probably an elephant," said Brian with a heavy stab at humour.

"It's big," replied Flower ominously.

Another step – but this time they said nothing. Then, compelled to turn by some instinct, Tim gasped with horrified amazement. A gorilla was standing in the undergrowth, watching them. He was enormous, with dark shaggy hair and a massive head with a kind of bony crest on his forehead. His eyes were large and inquisitive and there was something in them that told Tim not to move. Without looking at the others he knew instinctively that they had half-turned and were also watching the gorilla. Suddenly he began to make a strange, mournful hooting sound and Tim shivered. It was one of the most extra-ordinary sounds he had ever heard, for there was a kind of primitive human note to it. The gorilla cupped his hands and began to beat at his chest, which produced a hollow booming sound. This went on for some time, and then equally suddenly he stopped, standing completely silently, still watching them intently.

"Don't move," said Tim. "Just don't *do* anything."

The gorilla continued to scrutinise them for another few minutes. Then he lumbered away. No one spoke until he was lost in the undergrowth and they could no longer hear the slightest sound of his footsteps.

They stood up, almost in respect.

"That was incredible!" breathed Tim. "He was amazing!"

"What was he doing?"

"Just watching us," said Flower. "He's probably got children somewhere nearby." She spoke with a strange warmth, as if she completely understood the gorilla's lone appearance, and she certainly didn't seem in the least afraid. There was something else, thought Tim: Flower looked as refreshed as he suddenly felt – as if the appearance of the enormous, watchful animal had given them all new strength.

Chapter Five

For the next hour they climbed faster. It's weird, thought Tim, the way he's affected us. It's as if we're all companions; as if when we were watching each other it wasn't with hostility but with caution; as if we both had something to protect. He walked more lightly and his feet didn't hurt nearly as much as they had done before. Suddenly Flower said:

"I think we're there."

The ground was levelling out into a plateau between the two volcanoes that were silhouetted on the horizon in the eerie light. There seemed much less noise now as they began to walk through a series of grassy glades.

"What's that?" asked Brian suddenly.

"Water," said Flower. "A stream."

Minutes later they were on its banks, walking under yellow-flowered trees that were draped as the others had been with lichen. Even in the moonlight the stream was crystal clear, and they knelt down beside it to drink. The water was cold and utterly delicious. When they had drunk their fill, they walked on towards a group of huts with corrugated iron rooves. As soon as they stopped walking, Tim realised how cold it was – he felt chilled to the core.

"Let's knock at this one," said Flower, hurriedly walking over to the hut in the centre.

"Knock?" asked Brian. "This isn't suburbia."

Certainly there wasn't anything to knock with, so Flower thundered on the door with her fists. The reaction was almost instantaneous, as if the person inside was used to responding quickly. Within seconds, the door was open and a man with tousled blonde hair was on the threshold. He was in his mid-thirties, clean shaven, tall and very thin.

"Green Watch?" he asked. "We were expecting you hours ago. I was just about to get a search party together. I couldn't make up my mind whether the plane was late – it often is – or if Alison had had a puncture . . ." his voice tailed away. "Where *is* Alison? And Dan?"

Brian explained in short, stark sentences and Tim watched the first shock waves spread over John Best's face.

"I'm going to radio up the park guards," he said immediately. "Come on in – you must be finished off. Directly I've done this I'll get up a rescue party for

Dan." He spoke quietly and decisively, but Tim could see that he was greatly distressed.

The room was wonderfully warm inside, with a calor gas burner and shelves of books that ran all the way down one wall. There were old canvas chairs, a battered sofa, a scrubbed table with an oil lamp on it and a desk on which sat the radio John was now grappling with.

"Come in Park Twelve. Come in Park Twelve. This is Baker Charlie."

The voice came out of considerable static. "This is Park Twelve receiving you."

"We have trouble. Alison's been taken by poachers somewhere around the base of route six. Can't be more accurate. She's been shot and wounded and so has Dan Rilanga. He's bivouacked a couple of hours on foot from here. I can bring him in if you can start a search and rescue operation. Over."

"I hear you, Baker Charlie. Anyone else involved?"

"Three kids. They got here on their own."

"I'm sending out all available patrols now. Over."

"Keep in touch, Emmie."

"Will do."

John took off his headphones and turned to them. "I'm going to send out some of my people." He paused. "Can you describe where you bivouacked him?"

"Can't we go with them?" Flower asked.

"No, you're all done in. Must have some food and

44

rest. Did you – did you leave any kind of marker?"

"No," said Brian. "We were afraid the poachers would find him."

"OK. Just explain to me again where you think you left him – landmarks – anything."

Brian, who had a better sense of geography then the others, began to tell him, and after a few minutes of intense listening and questions John pronounced himself satisfied.

"You're all in," he said again. "Make yourselves some tea; there's food in the kitchen and bunks in the next room. Get some rest."

"I won't sleep while he's still out there," said Tim, echoing everyone's thoughts.

John grinned, looking both friendly and understanding. "We'll find him," he assured them. "Don't worry. By the time you've had something to eat you'll sleep all right."

"*I* won't," said Flower indignantly. "Not till I know he's back safely."

"OK," said John with another grin, but she could see it was a forced one. He left abruptly and they went into the tiny but well-stocked kitchen to find food and drink.

As they prepared it, Flower said, "He's really suffering. He must love her so much."

"Not much like an explorer type, is he?" commented Brian as he opened a tin of beans. "He's more like a -- sort of doctor or something."

"He's a vet," observed Tim, cutting a slice of what looked like home baked bread and stuffing some of it into his mouth. "What are vets meant to look like?"

Brian began to laugh in an exhausted sort of way, but Flower disapproved. "I don't see what's so funny; not with Dan lying out there dying and Alison still kidnapped."

Put that way it did seem as if Brian shouldn't be laughing, but he continued until Tim found himself forced to join in. It was fatigue and desperation, he told himself, as he laughed uncontrollably, dropping some bread on the floor and stumbling about with an open tin of potatoes.

"Really, you two *are* babies," sniffed Flower, with added disapproval. "You take everything far too lightly. I shall make John and his people coffee and wait up till they get back."

Half an hour later, all three members of Green Watch were asleep in their chairs, half empty plates around them.

"What's the time?"

"Eh?"

"The *time*?"

"What?"

"The time, you raving idiot!"

Tim jerked himself awake to find Flower looming over him like an angry goddess, looking both tired and bad-tempered.

"Eleven."

Sun was streaming through the windows and both the fire and the lamp had been switched off. Then

46

Tim found there was a pillow behind his head. Someone had been in here, looking after them, or had it been Flower?

"Thanks for the pillow," he said.

"What pillow?"

"This one – you put one behind Brian's head too. Have you had any sleep?" he asked sympathetically.

Briskly she told him to shut up, and when Tim looked up at her in surprise she snapped, "I fell asleep."

"Oh."

"I didn't want to – but I did."

Just then, Brian woke up. "Flower—"

"Well?" Her tone was ominous and Tim watched Brian put his foot well and truly in it.

"You been awake all night? Thanks for the—"

"Why don't you shut up!" she repeated bitterly.

John came in half an hour later when they had had a wash and made some coffee. All of them had been desperate to find out what had happened but, for some inexplicable reason, none of them could make up their minds to go outside.

"Are you all OK?" John looked tired and very strained.

"Fine," said Tim.

"I'm sorry to have—"

"Dan?" asked Flower. "I meant to wait up. Have you found him?"

"Yes, he's got a high fever but I've managed to remove the bullet."

47

"Will he be OK?" she persisted.

"If it hadn't been for you, he'd be dead," said John simply.

Brian wasn't having any of that. "He led us, you know."

"And if you hadn't been with him, he might not have had the need to keep going. At least – that's what he said."

"Is he going to be all right?" said Tim eagerly.

"I think he'll make it," said John slowly. "But he's in a bad state."

"Can't we get him air-lifted off?" asked Tim rather vaguely.

"The helicopters are out looking for Alison," he said. "But if he takes a turn for the worse they'll get him out. At the moment it's the fear not the bullet that matters." John paused. "He's being cared for by a remarkable young man named Malu. Actually he's Dan's son, and he knows a lot about medicine – orthodox and otherwise."

"What does that mean?" asked Flower.

"You'll find out. I'm going to leave you in his charge for a day. Maybe a couple of days."

Tim felt a sickening plunge in his stomach. Not again, he thought. Just as we're feeling a bit safer, it's all taken away again.

"Where are you going?" asked Flower uneasily. But of course she knew.

"To join in the hunt for Alison," he said bleakly.

"There's no news?"

"Not a thing." He hesitated. "I don't want to leave

you here, but the patrols – they're pretty thin on the ground and there's not a lot of people power – not for a hunt like this."

Brian nodded. "Can't *we* help?"

"It's too dodgy. These poachers – they can be very unpredictable."

"Why have they taken her?" asked Flower. "I mean – it seems so risky."

"It's to do with the gorillas."

"How?"

"She's – well, we're both getting the laws tightened up on protecting them. At the moment the gorillas are being driven higher and higher up the mountains, and the cold and the wet's really getting to them and making them ill. We're campaigning for more patrols – more arrests – so that in the end it's just not worth the poachers' while."

"I still don't see why they've taken her."

John looked grim. "If she was out of the way, then there'd just be me. And if *I* wasn't around . . ."

"You mean they'd kill her?" gasped Tim.

"They might. On the other hand if they *were* going to kill her, they'd have done it there and then, when they first captured her. I can only suppose they're holding her for a reason; maybe trying to get her to promise to leave them alone."

"She'd never do that," said Flower.

"Would she?" questioned Brian.

"No, but they could use pressure, or give her a warning. Either way, they've got her and there just aren't enough patrols to catch poachers let alone

49

rescue my wife. I've got to go. I've wasted too much time already." He turned as someone knocked on the door. "That'll be Malu. Come in!"

Malu was very young – only about nineteen – and he was short and muscular. He had something of his father's grave smile and there was a maturity to him that they all found reassuring.

"How is your father?" asked John.

"The same. Will you take everyone?"

"Is your mother here?"

"She come from the village. Be here in an hour."

"OK, Malu. Look after them. They're good."

"My father owes them his life," he said with a slow smile that flooded his face with warmth and a special kind of sincerity, as if he was already regarding them as equals rather than kids to be looked after and who might be a liability.

"Do you think so?" asked Flower. "I would have said we owed him ours."

Chapter Six

The base camp was like a paradise garden in the daylight. The stream was crystal clear, the pebbles on its bed polished and sparkling, while the lush grass, the lichen-hung trees and the fresh smell of earth and water all combined to make Flower, Brian and Tim feel revitalised.

When they went to see Dan he seemed peaceful, although the perspiration was running down his face in rivulets. His wife had arrived – a middle-aged, fine-boned and handsome woman who was shy and said little to Green Watch but a very great deal to Malu. In fact she rattled on at him in her own language for what seemed like ages, and it wasn't until they were out of the increasingly claustrophobic sick bay that Malu said, "She thinks he will get

better; that she can nurse him and he will get better."
He seemed very sure, and none of the three liked to
say anything although Dan looked far from well.

"Would you like to see them?" he asked.

"See who?" Flower stared at him, her mind still on
his father's sweating face.

"Group Two."

"Sorry?"

"Gorillas."

"Great," said Flower.

"Let me tell you some things first – just for
everyone's safety. There's Albert – he's the leader,
and Helena – that's his chief mate and her three
children, Sampson, Juniper and Jocasta. Then there's
his second mate, Sylvia, with her baby Tommy."

They didn't like to tell him that they already knew
the names of the gorillas in Group Two, so Brian told
Malu about their night-time visitor. "Was that
Albert, do you think?"

"No, it was probably Angus – he's a loner."

"You mean he doesn't have a family?"

"Never has had – he just roams around. We call
him the guardian because he seems to patrol and to
alert the other groups to any danger. Like poachers.
He was probably just checking you out."

"He made a kind of hooting sound, and then he
started to beat his chest," said Tim. "It was really
scary."

"And interesting," put in Brian, always the aca-
demic.

"How many groups are there?" asked Flower.

"Only about six; they're increasing in numbers but there's not enough forest left to support many more. The population in Rwanda's increasing, so more farmland's needed and the forest gets chopped down." Malu paused. "But what really started making life difficult for the gorillas happened about twenty years ago when we began growing pyrethrum flowers."

"Aren't those the ones that look like daisies?" asked Brian. "We passed a field of them as we came up."

"Yes. They contain a special chemical that can kill insects and Rwanda got a lot of money from European countries to cut down the forest in the National Park to grow them. We must have lost about forty per cent of the trees and the whole thing turned out to be a fiasco."

"Why's that?" asked Tim impatiently. He wanted to get on and see the gorillas, not listen to a lecture. But Brian was looking interested and Tim realised gloomily that he was bound to ask questions.

"Hundreds of families moved here, and each one was given a small plot of land to grow food and pyrethrum. One of these families was us." For a moment he looked very angry and Tim's interest returned. "Unfortunately, a few years after the beginning of the project, European scientists discovered how to make pyrethrum from chemicals, so our crops were not needed. We lost everything; the Park lost 100 square kilometres of forest and, worse still, they were on the warm lower slopes of the mountains. The land of the gorilla." He paused.

"How did you survive?" asked Tim.

"Scratch farming, but Dad had always loved the gorillas, and when the Mountain Gorillas Project was set up, he joined it. Then we met the Bests. I work for them, like Dad, as a guide. We bring tourists up to see the gorillas and that helps to pay for what we're doing."

Tim felt reassured. If tourists were taken to see the gorillas they couldn't be *that* dangerous. Then he thought of something. "Don't the tourists pass on germs to them?"

Malu nodded. "They sometimes pick up 'flu, but at least in the tourist season there are so many people up here, what with the guides and trackers, that it's much more difficult for the poachers." He paused again. "Look, the group we're going to, the leader – Albert – he doesn't like strangers and he might be a bit aggressive."

"Oh yes?" asked Tim warily.

"He may charge."

"What do we do? Run for it?"

"No," said Flower. "Don't you remember what Alison said?"

"Definitely not," agreed Malu. "He's only showing off – and he's nervous because Jocasta got caught in a snare and it's damaged her leg. Luckily it looks as if it's healing, so she's going to be OK. But they're not in familiar territory; they've been driven further up the mountain by the poachers, so they're a bit uncertain."

"Particularly Albert?" said Tim uneasily.

"Yes, so if he charges don't get up and run, whatever you do. He's just showing you he's the boss; you have to remember he's got the whole group to protect."

"But you'll be protecting us," said Brian quietly.

"Of course. One other thing—"

"Yes?" said Flower warily.

"Don't make eye contact with him – or any of them. They'll think it's a challenge."

"I'm not challenging anyone," said Tim firmly. "So I shan't be looking at them that closely."

They walked a little way out of the glades and struck across country, with Malu leading the way and Tim bringing up the rear. It was midday and the sun was high in the sky. Despite the fact that he had given them sun-hats the sweat was soon pouring off everyone but Malu, on whom it only glistened slightly at the nape of his neck. Suddenly he stopped and put a finger to his lips.

"Take it easy now," he whispered. "Just walk quietly."

They were moving along a single track that looked like a freshly made path, with frequent piles of dung. "This is a feeding trail," Malu said. "And the knuckle-prints in the mud – you can see which way they're travelling from those."

They pushed on for another ten minutes and then Malu motioned them to stop again. "They're very near," he said. "Slow up and follow me." They rounded a corner and stopped dead. They were here. Group Two – all asleep. At least that's the way it looked.

Tim, Flower and Brian froze, staring in awe at the huge slumbering animals. Big leafy branches had been used to make beds round a group of the old hagenia trees. Some of the nests had been made in forked branches. Tim counted six gorillas – two of them fully grown, three half grown and one very small, nestling in its mother's arms. There was an air of great tranquillity as the creatures slept. Then a head bobbed into view. It was very large, with massive canine teeth and its lips were parted in a look of anxiety. The anxiety quickly turned to aggression. Stand your ground. Don't look him in the eye, Tim told himself. This must be Albert.

"Do what I do," said Malu. "No jerky movements – just relax. Don't go near and stay behind me. And don't mind Albert."

It's hard to ignore him, thought Tim, for Albert was slowly standing up and that seemed pretty ominous. Maybe he was just asserting himself, but he definitely looked as if he was going to do rather more than that. Then Tim glanced at Malu and choked back a wild laugh, for he was hunched up on the ground grooming himself, picking and preening for all he was worth. He beckoned urgently for the others to squat down on their haunches. "Copy me," he hissed. Self-consciously they did as he told them, and it wasn't long before all three members of Green Watch were carefully grooming themselves, with gathering self-confidence. Then Malu broke off the stem of a plant from the undergrowth.

"It's wild celery," he said. "Eat it – it's good."

Again they did as he showed them, holding the celery in both hands and sucking and nibbling at it. Tim saw the other two were taking it all very seriously, and although he wanted to as well he still had an overpowering urge to laugh and go on laughing. Then he saw that all the gorillas' eyes were open – including the baby's – and they were watching their human imitators with interest while Albert stood uncertainly on two legs. At last, with a grunt, he fell back on to all fours, plucked some wild celery out of the foliage and began to munch at it. But his watchful eyes never left them.

Tim felt the magic slowly begin and the desire to laugh completely faded away, so much so that he was amazed that he had ever wanted to do so in the first place. He wanted to be part of it – he wanted to feel at one with the gorillas. As they woke and became more active he gradually began to identify them. Albert, the leader, appeased and feeling safe, watched over his flock with a calm wariness, his eyes rarely leaving them except to scan the surrounding undergrowth.

Sylvia, with her baby Tommy hanging on to her neck, was breaking open a giant plant of some kind with her fingers, scraping the white interior with her teeth and plucking out little morsels to pass up to Tommy, who regarded everything she was doing with intensely greedy eyes. It was easy to pick out Jocasta; the great wound on her foot must once have been very raw but it was now closing up and looked quite clean. Once the three children had eaten a few thistles they began to play, chasing each other up trees with a strange chuckling, barking sound, leaping from branch to branch and bringing down showers of leaves and moss and lichen. The noise finally woke Helena, who stretched and watched the three young gorillas occasionally land on the ground in mock fights. After a few of these, she reached out a lethargic hand and grabbed at Sampson – or was it Juniper? Tim wondered. She hugged the small gorilla to her while Jocasta ran over to Albert who also grabbed and hugged her. Then they all began feeding again.

Tim sat back, moved beyond anything he had felt before by the family atmosphere and the playful affection of Group Two. He looked at Jocasta's mangled foot and shuddered; how could anyone do this to them, even by accident? A great anger seized him and he forgot all about his fears and insecurities and the strangeness of the countryside. These creatures, however strong they were, were helpless in the face of the erosion and invasion of their homeland.

Suddenly the crack of a shot sounded from somewhere further down the mountain. Instantly the feeding came to a halt and Albert rose to his full height again. He looked round the trees and then his eyes fell on Brian. Brian stared back at him hypnotically as Albert began to drum on his chest.

"Stay where you are," whispered Malu. "Whatever you do, don't move."

Brian continued to stare up at Albert, his eyes rigidly fixed on him as if mesmerised.

"Now, start taking your eyes off him."

"I can't."

"Slowly take your eyes off him."

"I can't!" stuttered Brian. "He'll go for me!"

"He'll attack you if you don't." Malu's whisper was now an urgent hiss. "You *must* take your eyes off him! Now!"

"I can't."

"Now!"

Brian nodded and dragged his eyes away from Albert's. Tim relaxed a little, his muscles screaming.

"Stay where you are," Malu whispered, casually chewing on the wild celery. "That applies to everybody."

There was a long, unbearably tense pause while Albert stopped beating his chest but stayed upright, looking round the undergrowth suspiciously. The other gorillas huddled together, Sylvia clasping Tommy, all of them looking up at Albert. It was only then that Tim realised the full burden of the huge gorilla's responsibilities. Suddenly another shot cracked out in the valley, and to Tim's horror, he saw that Brian was staring hypnotically up at Albert again – and their eyes had met.

"What are you *doing*?" hissed Malu.

"I can't help it."

"You're crazy. Get your eyes away!"

"I *can't*."

"Now!"

"I *can't*!"

"Don't be a fool!" For the first time Malu's voice took on a desperate note as Albert began to lumber purposefully towards Brian.

"Get your eyes down." Flower's voice was low and insistent. "Get them down *now*."

"I can't."

"*Now*!"

And for the second time Brian managed to wrench his eyes away.

"Thank goodness!" muttered Malu.

Albert hesitated, but then he began to move towards Brian again drumming his chest fiercely.

"Now keep your eyes down – and wait till he gets a bit calmer."

Tim suddenly realised that Albert was in some way linking the disturbing shots lower down the mountain with Brian, and thought that by making eye contact with him in this way, Brian was challenging him.

"Don't move." Malu picked up another celery stalk and began to chew on it. "Everyone eat and relax."

Albert was now a few metres away from Brian, still drumming vigorously.

"Eat and relax, Brian."

"I *can't*," sobbed Brian.

"You must. Do it *now*!" Malu's voice was quietly authoritative.

Brian tried to break off a plant, but it was tough and wouldn't snap. Albert began barking aggressively as Brian tried and failed to break it. He grabbed at another, but Albert's barking grew louder. Tim was rigid with tension, his teeth and hands clenched, and when he looked across at Flower he could see that she was staring at Brian in agony.

Then Brian did the worst possible thing he could have done: he stumbled to his feet and froze.

"Sit down."

Brian remained motionless.

"I *said* – sit down." Malu's voice was commanding but clearly not commanding enough, for Brian stayed exactly where he was.

Meanwhile, Albert had stopped drumming and barking and was standing as motionless as Brian, with the other gorillas huddled behind him. Doesn't he realise – Tim's thoughts pounded away – doesn't he realise that Albert is now seeing him as an enemy, as someone who could wipe out his beloved family?

"Sit down," said Flower.

"Please—" Malu's voice shook.

But Brian was driven by fear and Tim knew he was beyond reason.

Then Albert hooted and Brian, with a sobbing

gasp, turned and burst into a run. With long easy strides but beginning to bark again, Albert set off in pursuit.

"Brian!"

"Don't shout, Flower," hissed Malu.

"Brian—"

"Shut up!"

The chase was a short one for Brian tripped and fell, lying on the ground, his eyes closed, while Albert stood over him with a paw raised threateningly.

Then Malu was on his feet, dashing over to Albert, making a weird chuckling noise, leaping, dancing, playing – turning it all into a game. Would Albert accept this ruse? wondered Tim. It didn't look as if it had a chance as Malu circled Albert with his strange sounds and playful gestures. Albert turned, hesitated, turned back to the prone Brian, hesitated and then turned again to Malu. Then he went down on all fours and charged straight at him.

Malu dodged, feinted and dodged again while Albert lumbered straight past him and stopped. Then Malu picked up a thistle and began to pull it apart, ready for eating. Slowly, Albert began to do the same.

"Roll over, Brian – quietly," said Malu, eating his thistle.

Albert chewed appreciatively.

"Now." Malu's voice was still very gentle.

Brian didn't move.

"Now!"

Slowly Brian rolled over and got to his feet.

"Walk slowly back to your friends."

Numbly Brian did as he was told.

Slowly, very slowly, they all withdrew into the trees, leaving the gorillas crouched together.

"He'll move them on in a minute," said Malu as they walked back down the feeding trail. "Thank goodness there weren't any more shots."

"I'm sorry," said Brian brokenly. "I'm really sorry."

Malu went up to him and put his arm round him. "It doesn't matter."

"It does," replied Brian fiercely.

"It's all a matter of experience – you have to learn."

"The others didn't need to." His voice shook.

"They were lucky. These great beasts draw your eyes up – I know how it feels." Malu paused. "I've done it myself."

'You have?"

"Years ago. You only do it once. I didn't get off as lightly as you did."

"What happened?"

"One of them – the leader – came along and hit me. He broke my arm. I was lucky my father was there to do what I did today."

"You saved my life."

"I just distracted him – that's all."

"You still saved my life," said Brian slowly.

"Maybe – but now you know. However much you want to look them in the eye, don't."

"I'll remember all right." But he was feeling a bit better about it now.

They all walked back to the base in companionable silence. Tim was very moved. Now that Brian was safe, and the horrible part was over, he was able to appreciate the time they had shared with these extraordinary creatures. They were so human – so near to him. Well, he thought, we are related – they are the beginnings of man. But it wasn't so much that that had entranced him, it was their vulnerability. For such massively strong animals, he had never realised how exposed they were, so much at risk. And there was something beyond all that. He had shared with them and been temporarily, very temporarily, accepted. And that had been the most wonderful feeling he had ever experienced.

Chapter Seven

"Where did those shots come from?" asked Flower as they sat in the late afternoon sun eating a delicious vegetable stew that Malu's mother had prepared. The stream rushed past their feet and they felt completely relaxed, both mentally and physically. Dan was much the same; the fever was still with him, but at least he seemed to be sleeping.

"A couple of kilometres below us," said Malu. "But they weren't necessarily the same poachers who took Alison. There are increasing numbers of them and they're often just villagers in need of meat. Their farms still don't really produce enough for them to live on and there aren't enough patrols to stop them."

"Are we going to see the gorillas again?" asked Brian quietly.

"Of course we are," Malu replied. "We'll find them again tomorrow, but with those hunters about they'll probably move further up the mountain."

Green Watch spent the remainder of the day resting and playing a game rather like bowls that Malu taught them. Later they sat by the stream and watched a magnificent sunset. As the sun rapidly sank down in a bank of blazing crimson light, Flower suddenly said:

"What are they doing to her?"

"She'll be all right," Tim replied too quickly. "They only want her as a hostage or something."

"Don't be such an idiot!" she snapped. "You're not thinking it through at all; all you can think of is those overgrown monkeys. I can't sit here and do nothing."

"John's out looking – and the patrols," replied Brian, knowing that he sounded equally feeble. "What else could we do?"

"Anything but sit here," she said sharply. "What's that?"

"Eh?" Tim looked round but he couldn't see anything.

"I saw something, like a – a tiger." Her voice faltered.

"It couldn't have been," Brian snapped. "You know perfectly well there're no tigers in Africa."

"It was something. Something striped." She was insistent.

"Just a—"

"Look. There it is again. Right over there in those trees."

Brian and Tim looked hard, but they couldn't see anything. Then they were startled rigid as a single drum began to beat.

"Where is it?" whispered Flower.

"What?" asked Tim.

"The drum, you idiot!"

"It could be a long way away," said Brian.

But Flower wasn't so sure. "It feels near."

They all stared into the dense undergrowth but there was no sign of anyone now.

"Where are you?" It was Malu's voice, calling anxiously from over by the huts. They got up shakily and ran to join him.

"What's going on?" asked Brian.

"Nothing."

"But the drum – and Flower thought she saw something – something striped – in the trees."

Malu looked worried. "You'd better come in—"

But before he had a chance to say any more there was a dreadful sound – a sort of long-drawn-out screech which seemed to go on and on. Then it stopped – and began again on a slightly lower but no less frightening note.

"What's *that*?" said Flower, wide-eyed with fear.

Malu looked dazed, as if someone had punched him very hard and very suddenly. For a few seconds he said nothing.

"What *is* it?" repeated Flower, almost angrily.

"It's a gorilla," he said. "And he's in trouble." He grabbed a rifle and tried to push past them but they all stood their ground.

"You're not going anywhere," said Tim, surprising himself with his own boldness. "Not till we know what's going on." He was desperate and he knew the others were too. They just couldn't be deserted again.

"It's a gorilla – caught in a trap. And it sounds like a male adult. I've got to go."

"We're coming!" said Brian determinedly.

"Then you'll have to keep up," said Malu curtly, hoping they wouldn't hamper him too much.

He ran lightly and the others followed, stumbling, until he turned and said, "Run with big strides – run as if you're flying." But unseen obstacles in the darkness sent them crashing down, one after the other, and although they picked themselves up, they felt bruised and stupid. Several times they lost sight of him, but always caught a glimpse of him in the end. The single drumming had stopped with the screeching, but that terrible sound increased almost without interruption. They drew nearer to the source of the pain and eventually arrived in a small clearing. Hanging high above them by one leg that was firmly caught in the snare was a huge gorilla who beat at the air and shrilled with a dreadful agony. He was vaguely familiar.

Eventually Tim breathed, "Isn't that Angus?"

"Yes, the loner."

"He was the guardian," said Flower, the tears pouring down her cheeks.

"Yes," replied Malu bitterly. "Maybe they knew it."

"Did he just walk into it, or—"

"It's pretty strong looking," said Malu angrily. "Far too strong for bushbuck. They must have been after him."

"For God's sake get him down!" said Flower as the huge animal threshed and howled above them.

"It's Tanner's work, I'm sure of it." Malu sounded as if he was talking to himself. "But I thought he was dead – I *knew* he was dead."

"Who's Tanner?" asked Tim.

But Malu was still thinking aloud. "It's beginning to explain a lot," he muttered.

"For God's sake get him down!" yelled Flower above Angus's screams.

Malu laid down his gun and took from his belt a sharp, curved knife. He slashed at Angus's bonds and the gorilla fell to the ground with a huge, dull thump. For a while he lay on his back, his eyes staring up at them in a mixture of relief and abject misery.

"His foot's bad," said Malu, looking cautiously down at the mangled, pulpy mass.

"Can't you bind it up?" asked Tim.

"He wouldn't tolerate that. He'll clean it and bathe it himself. But if it goes septic—"

"What happens then?" asked Flower threateningly.

"John would use a tranquilliser dart and put him

out for a bit. Then he'd clean and dress it."

"John isn't here." said Brian woodenly.

"He'll be back."

Angus suddenly turned over and staggered away on all fours. Once or twice he looked back, staring at them accusingly. Tim had the feeling that he was wondering whether they were rescuers or enemies.

"OK," said Brian. "Who's Tanner?"

Malu hesitated. Then he began to speak very quickly. "Tanner was a guide here a few years ago. He's a white man with a lot of problems – drink was one of them. I think he'd originally been a naturalist. Anyway, he knew the park well and was useful enough at first. Then he began to take an interest in the souvenir trade."

"Souvenirs?"

"Yes." Malu spoke slowly and painfully. "Skins, skulls, hands turned into ashtrays . . . . He's made a fortune out of slaughtering gorillas over the last few years, and he's too experienced a tracker to let the patrols catch him. He's also organised the poachers into more efficient groups and I'm sure he was taking a cut on the bushbuck skins."

They all listened intently, knowing there was more to come and none of it was going to be nice.

"He's been counter-attacked by the gorillas a couple of times; it's as if they know he's their worst enemy. Tanner began to hate them as much as they seem to hate him. I know that on one occasion he came up here with a gun and my dad took it off him. The Bests dismissed him and we had to guard the

70

group for months; several times he came near to killing them. His drinking became much heavier as well. But he hasn't been around for a while and I was told he'd drowned, canoeing further down the valley."

"One trap doesn't prove much," said Brian.

"Maybe not. But he used to wind us up – and the gorillas. They're terrified of those single drum beats. He used to play that drum all over the bush. He knew we'd never find him and he used to pound that drum for hours. Then he'd come in, with his trap and rifle."

"Do you reckon it was him who took Alison? Maybe he's in league with the poachers who kidnapped her."

"I don't know—" Malu looked uneasy.

"If you do know anything you must say," said Flower.

"All I know is that there *could* be a reason—"

"What?"

"He hated John and Alison because they protected the gorillas."

"Why would he have gone away and then come back again?" asked Tim. "Even supposing the report about him drowning was untrue."

"I don't know. Maybe – maybe he's determined to start up all over again."

"Do you know where he might be hanging out?"

"No." But there was something in his voice that made Flower want to probe further.

"You sure?"

"I know where he used to live."

71

"Where?" she insisted.

"There's a plane. It crashed here years ago. He used to camp out in part of the fuselage. But—"

"Where is it now?"

"Above a waterfall. Quite a way from here." He sounded more positive now.

"Shouldn't we go there?"

"You bet we should!" Malu said with sudden alacrity. "But you have to realise something: if George Tanner *is* alive, then he's bound to be more dangerous than ever."

That night, they sat round the fire in John's hut and talked to Malu about the coming day. Each member of Green Watch was insistent that they should come on the trek to the waterfall, while Malu was equally insistent that they did not.

"I am responsible for you here," he said. "How can you expect me to lead you into such a place? If George Tanner is still alive, and connected with the kidnap, he's not going to be somebody who'll negotiate with us. What would your parents say?"

"My father would say – go right in. We've been in danger before."

"Not this kind," said Malu stubbornly.

The argument continued with neither side giving an inch until Brian finally said, "If you don't let us go with you, we'll follow."

"I shall travel too fast."

"Then we'll get lost."

Malu took a long look at their completely adamant faces. "Listen it's your decision."

"We know that," said Flower quietly.

"You have to do what I say."

"If we think it's right," she replied, "we'll do what you say."

Tim lay awake, listening to the night sounds, thinking about everything that had happened to them since they arrived in Africa. Kidnappings, shootings, traps, unpredictable gorillas and now the mysterious Tanner – it was all much worse than anything they had ever had to face before. He looked across at Brian, but he seemed to be fast asleep. Was Flower able to slip out of wakefulness so easily, just like that? Anyway, he couldn't; there seemed to be an immense gulf between lying awake and the possibility of ever sleeping again.

In the end Tim couldn't bear the sheer boredom of lying in bed any longer. Fumbling his way to the window, he peered out at the clearing, now sharply etched in the moonlight. The stream looked like thin, translucent milk and the grass had a strange, almost frosty glow to it. For a moment Tim wondered if he had slept after all and was dreaming. The clearing seemed transformed – almost magical. He felt the hard edge of the window-sill. He was awake all right – he could even smell the onions they had had for supper.

Then he gave a gasp of surprise and went rigid. There was a figure in the clearing and it seemed to be gazing straight at him. Tim wondered if he could be seen; he was not standing in the centre of the window, but a bit to the side. The figure was amazing. It was a man; he was very tall and quite old, but he was wearing only a pair of shorts, and his entire body, including his face, was painted in stripes. It was difficult to see their colour in the moonlight but they gave a snake-like impression to his body. Could this be the crazy Tanner? But hadn't Malu said he was white? This man was definitely black, or was he? Could the stripes have given that effect?

Somehow Tim tore himself away from his position by the window and crept into the other room where Malu was sleeping in a camp bed – or should have been. The sheets were turned back and the bed was cold.

Tim debated whether or not to wake the others. Then he heard a slight thudding sound and he stole to the next window. A shadow detached itself from somewhere by the stream and began to walk softly past. It was Malu.

Chapter Eight

Consumed with curiosity, Tim thought rapidly. Surely it would be safe outside if Malu was there? He opened the door quietly and stepped out into the night. Looking around, he saw no one and everything was still, so he crept in the direction the others had taken. The moon went behind a cloud and he stumbled, giving out a little cry of surprise. He stood there tensely, hoping he had not been heard and knowing he should have stayed inside the hut. A little night wind, chill and darting, ran through his hair making him shiver, but eventually he tiptoed on. Then he saw them – round the back of one of the huts, crouched down together: the painted man, Malu and a large gorilla. It was impossible! Yet there they were. His foot cracked on something and the painted man looked up immediately. The moon rode out from behind the cloud to reveal the old man's lividly painted face and a row of yellow, heavily stained teeth. Malu looked up a few seconds later and whispered, "Tim?"

"What are you doing?"

"What are *you* doing?" Malu retorted.

"I heard a noise – saw a figure."

The gorilla rose to its feet. Amazed, Tim realised it was a man – or was it a woman? – wearing a mask – an extremely realistic gorilla mask. Then the mask was pulled off and Tim saw the face of Malu's mother underneath.

"Don't worry, Tim," Malu said softly. "There's nothing to be afraid of."

"I don't believe it," muttered Tim. "Why?"

The painted man began to chatter at Malu and then at his mother. Malu spoke to him quickly and he said no more, but his huge eyes never left Tim's face.

"I can explain," said Malu, getting to his feet.

"Explain?"

"You want an explanation, don't you?"

Tim simply stared back at him. "Why's your mother dressed up in a gorilla mask?" he said eventually. It seemed utterly ludicrous.

Malu turned away. "You'll laugh. I know you'll laugh."

"I'm not like that," said Tim simply and Malu could feel the sincerity in his voice.

"We've been practising our medicine."

"What for?" he said at last.

76

"My father is worse," he said sadly.

"How much worse?"

"We're really worried about him."

"Can't you get a helicopter?" asked Tim desperately, conscious of their isolation without any adult support.

"They can't come till tomorrow – they're both out. One's dealing with a fire; the other's got engine trouble."

"You think he'll – die tonight?"

"He might," said Malu. "So we try *our* medicine."

"I don't understand."

"When you do, you'll laugh," said Malu again.

"Did John laugh – if he ever saw this?"

"No – and he did."

"Did Alison?"

"No."

"Then why should I?"

"You don't understand Africa," he said stubbornly.

"I never will if you don't help me," said Tim miserably. For a moment there was understanding in Malu's eyes and Tim pressed home his advantage. "What are you doing? Who is the painted man? And why was your mother wearing that mask?"

"The painted man is Bailu; he's what you would call a witch-doctor and we'd call a wise man. A herbalist."

"And the mask?"

"She was wearing that because, to our tribe, the head is sacred. He – my father – must touch it while he drinks what Balu is making."

"What is he making?"

"A potion."

"Will it work?"

"It's worked on my people before," said Malu. He paused suspiciously, looking at Tim intently. Tim knew why.

"Am I laughing?" he said.

"Not yet," admitted Malu grudgingly. "Perhaps you will laugh when you return to your friends."

"No. When will you give it to your father? The potion?"

"Now."

"Can I come?"

"If you wish. But you mustn't ask questions."

"Can I ask one now?"

"What is it?" Malu said impatiently.

"Is your – magic – very old?"

"Yes," he said. "It was here hundreds of years before your medicine. We had to rely on it once. A lot of us still do."

Dan had certainly taken a turn for the worse. He was throwing himself about and the sweat was pouring off him. Bailu, Malu and his mother gathered round his bed, while Tim stood back. Somehow, instead of looking crazy in her gorilla mask, Malu's mother seemed tender and loving. Bailu began chanting, holding a beaker of the potion over Dan's head. The chanting was hypnotic and seemed to go on forever. Then the woman sat beside Dan's bed and began to

78

stroke his forehead. After a while his hand reached up searchingly and he began, in his turn, to stroke the gorilla fur on the mask.

Malu turned back to Tim. "This will go on for some time," he said.

"He looks calmer."

"Yes."

"Will it work?"

"It might. It's like your medicine – it's not infallible. Sometimes it doesn't work at all."

"But sometimes it does? It has worked?"

"Like your medicine, yes."

The chanting and stroking continued for another few minutes, then Tim saw Malu stiffen.

"What's up?"

"Look."

"Where?"

"There! In the shadows by the stream."

"It's – it's Angus! I can see him limping," exclaimed Tim excitedly. "Why's he here?"

"Well, he often does pay us a visit," said Malu slowly.

"But why now?" Tim was very excited.

"Just a coincidence."

"It can't be."

"You must make up your own mind," said Malu quietly.

"It's magic!"

"I never said that."

"It *must* be!"

"Why can't it be a coincidence?" asked Malu gently.

"Because he's the guardian."

Malu said nothing.

"Isn't he?"

"That's what they say."

"Is he better?" asked Tim urgently.

"He hasn't had much time – but he certainly looks better."

Angus looked up towards the hut and stared at the lighted window. Then he turned and looked away.

Dan lay back as the chanting ended. He seemed exhausted, but Malu moved forward and put his hand behind his head and lifted him up again.

"Drink it, Father."

Bailu held the beaker to Dan's mouth and then began to chant again. Slowly, Dan drank. When he had finished, Malu gently laid his head back on the pillow and kissed him tenderly on the forehead.

"I love you, Father."

"Mm."

"You have received the Aguna."

Dan's face gave a tired smile. "Good."

"You'll rest now, and a helicopter will be here in the morning to take you to hospital."

"No."

"You must go, Father."

"The medicine—"

"We must try *all* medicines." He took his hand gently and kissed it. "Come on outside," he said to Tim. "I'll leave Bailu and my mother with him."

They walked out into the cold, clear air. The volcanoes loomed above them; strands of mist streaked the moonlight.

"Why did you think I'd laugh?" asked Tim.

"Native mumbo-jumbo—"

"I don't think like that. This place is old."

Malu smiled.

"Have you ever been outside Africa?" Tim went on.

"No."

"But you speak English so well."

"You have to as a guide."

They were companionably silent, looking out at the forest.

"He's out there."

"Angus? Yes."

"Watching us?"

"I believe he *is* the guardian. But you probably think I'm superstitious."

"Don't talk like that," said Tim. "I believe in him too. But what would happen if they killed him – if George Tanner killed him? Turned bits of him into tourist souvenirs?"

"That's what I'm afraid of." Malu yawned. "I'll sit with my father now."

"Can't I?"

"No. If you're coming tomorrow you need all the sleep you can get."

Tim yawned too. "I reckon I'll sleep now."

"Good. It's going to be tough."

"Do you think Angus will come with us tomorrow?"

81

"He might. He's inclined to follow human beings. But then he's got the gorillas to look after. Now go."

"OK," said Tim reluctantly.

"Sleep well – and, Tim—"

"Yes?"

"Thanks."

"What for?"

"Believing."

Tim turned away. "I believe all right," he said.

Chapter Nine

"Get up."

Tim rolled over in bed.

"Tim."

He closed his eyes against the insistent voice.

"You've got to get up."

Tim sat up reluctantly and saw that it was Malu. He had a rucksack on his back.

"We've got fifteen minutes," he said. "Then we must go."

"What's the time?"

"Six."

Tim groaned.

"Get the others on their feet and grab some breakfast. I'll be outside."

"Wait."

"Yes?"

"How's Dan?"

"The helicopter will be here in a few minutes. The fever's better but I still don't like the look of the bullet wound. Anyway, he'll be at the hospital in half an hour and they'll look after him."

"How long's the journey?"

"It's a hard trek," he said evasively, "right round to the other side of the volcanoes. Of course, it could all be a waste of time —" His voice tailed away. "We'll have to see." Malu adjusted something at his belt and Tim could see that it was a holster. He scrambled out of bed and grabbed his clothes.

As they hurried through breakfast, Tim told Flower and Brian what had happened during the night.

"It's true," Flower said. "About alternative medicine and all that. I'm sure it does work."

"It needs to be backed up with the scientific stuff," said Brian, rather smugly.

"You might not be able to trust either on their own." Tim's voice was firm, but there was no time for any further discussion for suddenly they could hear the helicopter buzzing overhead.

When they came out, two paramedics were loading Dan into the machine by stretcher. They didn't stop longer than a few minutes and then the helicopter was airborne again, weaving its way above the treetops, up to a cloudless sky.

"It's going to be hot," said Malu rather gloomily as

he kissed his mother goodbye. Of the painted man there was no sign.

They trekked for two hours in gradually increasingly heat. Each member of the expedition had a rucksack, a couple of water bottles, limited food supplies and sharp curved knives called pangas, which were designed for hacking a path through the bush. They didn't take many regular trails, although it was a tremendous relief to be on one. Most of the time they hacked their way through dense vegetation while Malu guided them with his compass.

At about eight-thirty they stopped for a drink and a bar of chocolate.

"We have company," said Malu.

"Where?" Flower leapt up.

"Sit down – you'll disturb them."

"I thought you meant head-hunters or something," she said, reluctantly subsiding.

"We don't have them out here," laughed Malu. "I think they got invented for films. But we do have other company."

"Angus?" asked Tim.

"I think he's ahead of us, but Group Two are over there." He pointed vaguely into the bush.

"How do you know?" asked Brian curiously. "I haven't heard a sound."

"You must have," replied Malu. "You've heard dozens of sounds. They go on all the time; it's just a question of identifying the right ones."

"Are they following us?" asked Tim.

"Maybe. Hard to say."

"How do you know it isn't another group?" asked Tim.

"I've studied this group so much that I know Albert's hoots by now – just by the tone. And I could hear little Tommy chattering as well."

They moved on, walking fast, hacking their way through the bush for another hour. By now it was very hot indeed.

Suddenly Malu put a finger to his lips. "They're close," he said. They were on a trail now, but it was a fresh one, with the giant stinging nettles flattened and plants and shoots broken.

"Is this a feeding trail?" asked Brian.

"Looks like it," whispered Malu.

They were on them in seconds but this time no one was awake. Albert, Helena, Sampson, Juniper and Jocasta, Sylvia and Tommy were lying in the bush, eyes closed and chests slowly heaving in deep sleep. Something moved in the undergrowth and a big, dark shape peered from underneath one of the hagenia trees.

Malu motioned them back. "It's Angus," he said. "No wonder they're all sleeping so peacefully. The guardian's here."

Angus lumbered out and Albert opened one eye. Helena was asleep in the crook of his arm and he seemed loath to disturb her.

"Now – start eating something," said Malu, crouching down. "And don't make eye contact."

Tim cast a wary look at Brian but his eyes were firmly averted. Malu began to make a low huh-huh sound and Angus returned it, reaching up to a branch to pull something down and stuff it in his mouth.

Tim broke off some wild celery and tried to eat a piece, but his mouth was so dry he could only pretend, and he didn't dare open his water bottle for fear of offending the gorillas with such an alien action.

"Now back off slowly," said Malu softly. "They'll be here for some time yet and we can't afford to be as lazy as they are."

We can't move as fast either, thought Tim.

"It's good to know they're around," said Flower. "I feel safe."

"They wouldn't protect us," replied Malu. "But I know what you mean."

They walked on, the heat becoming more and more intense, and began to climb again.

"It's strange," said Malu later. "They're with us again."

As they walked on he taught them to listen out for the gorilla sounds, and soon they all began to identify the odd bark, hoot and chatter and, once, a startled shriek.

"Do they normally follow like this?" asked Flower.

"No, it's very unusual."

They climbed higher and Tim could feel the air getting thinner. Now they were on a gently sloping mountain path that ran through a canyon between the two peaks. Here, the trail broadened out.

"What's that?" asked Brian suddenly. "That rushing, thundering sound? Is it the waterfall?"

Malu nodded.

"And the plane?"

"We have to climb up beside the fall. That's the tough bit," he added, as if they weren't exhausted enough already.

As they neared the falls, they could see the spume of spray above the dense green treetops, and at last, turning a bend in the canyon, they saw the water pouring down the mountainside. The noise was so loud they could hardly hear themselves speak, and they stood still, entranced by its silvery power.

"It's wonderful," said Tim. "Magic."

There was nothing else to say; he had summed it up exactly.

"Where are the gorillas?" asked Brian.

Malu shook his head. "I can't hear them now because of the waterfall. We're going to climb up the side; it's not sheer – there's even a track – but if you're afraid of heights, don't look down. It's going to be difficult to speak up there so just keep going behind me."

They began to struggle up the steep, damp track, part rock and part slippery earth beside the waterfall. It was an exhausting, frustrating climb and Tim thought they would never reach the top. His mind slid back to the time when he'd first met Green Watch. He had thought then that he'd never conquer his fear of heights or be able to handle dangerous situations as well as the others did. It was different now, he thought. His adventures with them had improved his self-confidence beyond all recognition.

With their knives stuck in their belts and their rucksacks becoming intolerable burdens, all four sweated and strained their way up until at last they reached the top. Collapsing on a rock, they looked down at the massive scale of the falls and the clouds of mist that rose over it. Then Malu said: "I want you to keep your voices right down once we leave the falls behind. The plane is inland, near the river. I don't want anyone to hear us coming."

They began to walk by the side of the swiftly flowing river that made such a dramatic disappearance, dropping hundreds of metres over the falls. Tim watched some driftwood spin towards the drop and shuddered. There would be no way of preventing yourself from going over; the current was immense and the swollen brown river flowed at a fantastic speed. For the first time he began to feel very nervous, and looking at the others he could see all too clearly that they were feeling the same. Only Malu pounded on, seemingly oblivious to the danger they might be walking into.

"Wait." Malu stopped abruptly. "I thought I saw something. Get down."

They crouched down behind some bushes. The river was calmer here and the rush of water no longer so loud.

Tim peered through the bushes but couldn't see anything. "What was it?" he whispered.

"I'm not sure —"

"Where's the plane?" hissed Flower.

"Not far now."

"What are we going to do?"

"Wait for a bit. Then we'll cut up the hill and look down."

They waited and waited, but couldn't see anything. Eventually Malu signalled them on and they began to climb up the hillside, keeping low while the river broadened out below them and became even calmer. Then Tim saw the plane.

It was just the shell of a fuselage, and it was lying in a slight dip. There was no sign of habitation and the site looked totally derelict and deserted.

"I'm going down to take a look," said Malu.

"No you're not," said Flower. "That's how all the adults in our lives disappear."

Malu grinned fleetingly and then looked very stern. "I'm not doing a disappearing act." He pulled out a pair of field glasses. "Watch me through these."

Flower took them and looked down. "I can see everything quite clearly," she said. Turning towards the river she exclaimed. "Look – there's a fork in the river over there; it splits in two."

The others looked at it fleetingly and then stared back anxiously at the plane.

There was a long pause. Then Flower said, "Go on then, but be quick."

Without saying anything more, Malu checked his holster and began to weave his way down the hillside.

At last he was down there and Tim felt his stomach muscles tightening. Malu hesitated, stared through a window of the fuselage, paused and then darted round the other side. He re-emerged seconds later, looked up at Green Watch waiting anxiously on the hillside and shrugged. Then he stepped inside the plane through a hole in its side. It was as if he had suddenly been swallowed up by an enormous stranded whale.

"He's been gone a long time," said Tim.

"A minute so far," replied Brian with irritating steadiness.

"It seems a long time," snapped Tim.

"I wouldn't say a minute was —"

"Shut up!"

"All right, you two," said Flower. "Don't start arguing."

"Well," Tim's nerves were raw, "it's such a silly comment."

"I don't see why," began Brian. "All I said was —"

91

"Wait!" Flower crouched down even further, waving the others down too.

"What's up?" Tim hissed.

But they could see what was up all too clearly. A canoe was coming down the left-hand fork in the river. Fast.

"Don't shout." Flower grabbed Tim as he stood up. He sat down again quickly.

"Where on earth is he?" Brian stared down at the plane, willing Malu to come out.

"The canoe –" Tim said. "It's heading for – we've got to warn him."

"What's he *doing* in there?" whispered Brian. "What's keeping him so long?"

"*I* don't know." snapped Tim.

"You don't know anything, do you?" It was Brian's turn to be bad-tempered.

"Idiot!"

"Don't call *me* an idiot!"

"Be quiet, you two!" Flower was furious. "Just be quiet. Look the canoe's going upstream."

It was. The canoeist, still too indistinct to see, had turned at the fork and was going upstream now and paddling hard.

Tim prayed that Malu wouldn't come out – and he didn't. The canoeist rounded a bend and was lost to sight.

Almost immediately, Malu came out of the fuse-lage, looked around furtively and began to run up the hillside towards them, keeping as close to the ground as possible. He arrived panting, and threw himself down.

"I saw him."

"We were desperate," said Flower. "We thought you were coming out any moment."

"And I thought he was coming in."

"What's in there?" asked Tim.

"Nothing," said Malu. "Absolutely nothing at all."

There was a long silence. Everyone was depressed by the anticlimax.

"Nothing?" repeated Brian. "There must be something."

"Well, there wasn't. But that was George Tanner all right, I'm sure of it. He's older obviously, and grown a beard, but it's him."

Tim felt a shiver of apprehension. "Did he look dangerous?" he asked naïvely.

"No, he looked determined."

"Do you think he's living somewhere further up the river now?"

"Could be. We'll move on."

They trekked on round two enormous bends in the river, then Malu stopped.

"Hear that?"

They listened carefully.

"Hooting – sort of hooting."

"It's Angus."

"What's he doing up here?" said Brian wonder-ingly. "Do you think Group Two will be somewhere behind us as well?"

"They could be," said Malu. "It's a long way for them though."

"Maybe he's following us – guarding us?" sugges-ted Tim.

"No, we can't give gorillas human thoughts. But there's something that's drawn him up here, though I can't think what."

"Wait a minute – there's smoke up there, coming through the trees."

They saw a wisp and then another. Then as they came over a rise they saw the log hut by the side of the river. Very small, built on grass above a sandy shore, it looked idyllic – a retreat in paradise. There was no sign of a canoe or of any human being, but next to the hut was another smaller building with a grille across the front. Something was moving inside.

Malu brought out his field glasses and stared down for a long time. Then he said softly, "Now I see."

"What's down there?" asked Flower.

"He seems to have got something in that cage; I think it's a baby gorilla. No wonder Angus is here, and maybe Albert and his family *are* somewhere around."

"Would they know it was there? I mean we've come a long way," began Tim, but Malu seemed very sure.

"Oh yes," he said. "I don't know the extent of their instincts – but they're powerful. Far more powerful than we can ever imagine."

"Why has he got the gorilla down there?" asked Tim.

"Maybe it's there to attract other gorillas," said Brian thoughtfully. "So they're really playing into his hands. It's a trap – for all of them."

There was a long, startled silence.

Then Malu said, "Brian, I've got this dreadful feeling you could be right."

"We've got to warn them." Tim burst out, and then realised how absurd he was being. He looked away, feeling extremely stupid.

Malu took his arm. "It's Tanner we're after," he said. "We've got to stop him. Angus and the others are very near. They could go in at any moment. We've got to work something out fast." He looked down again with his glasses. "No!" he exclaimed.

"What have you seen?"

He passed Flower the glasses without saying anything. She looked, shuddered and passed them on to Brian. He said nothing either but Tim could see that he was very pale as he in turn handed over the field glasses. Tim took one look and that was enough: over the doorway of the hut that faced away from the river was the skull of a gorilla.

Chapter Ten

"Can't we ambush him?" Tim was close to tears in his anger. "There're four of us."

"He'll be armed," replied Malu.

"So are we; at least, you are."

"And don't forget he may have Alison as a hostage."

"So what are we going to do?" asked Tim impatiently.

"I'll go down —"

"No," said Flower determinedly. "We'll all go. And you'll not stop us this time."

Malu shrugged. "Very well, but you must do exactly what I say."

"Why don't we spread out –" began Brian.

"No!" Malu's voice was sharp. "I told you, he'll be

armed if he's there. We'll keep together." He took another look through his binoculars and said, "I don't see the canoe, but it could be anywhere. Or he could come back. So we go down very cautiously as a group. And we stay together."

"Can we release that baby gorilla?" asked Flower.

"If it's unharmed – yes."

"We can't let him keep it," she began.

"OK," said Malu, ignoring her and casting an anxious eye at the river. "Let's go."

Slowly and watchfully they inched their way down the hillside, the sun beating down on them relentlessly as they emerged from the trees. Eventually they reached the hut which seemed silent but watchful in the intense heat.

Malu gestured to the others to follow him as he skirted the front door, trying to ignore the gorilla skull. Looking into one of the windows Tim saw a neat, anonymous room with a bed, table, chair and bookcase. There were only half a dozen books on it and the whole space had a spartan, functional air as if the owner never relaxed, was always vigilant. On the beach there was nothing but sand and an old upturned rowing boat. Then they moved on to the baby gorilla which was silent and unfriendly, sitting on the floor of its cage, its huge eyes staring ahead. They wondered how long it had been there and how much human company it had had. It was impossible to tell of course; certainly the animal showed neither pleasure nor fear at seeing them.

"It just seems cowed," whispered Brian.

"As if it's had all its emotions beaten out of it," agreed Flower. Tim saw there was a dark anger in her eyes and he himself felt he could not speak at all without choking.

"OK," hissed Malu. "See where it's looking."

The baby gorilla's eyes were firmly fixed on the hillside.

"They must be up there," said Malu. "The others."

They all looked up but could see nothing.

"We *must* release it," demanded Flower.

Malu nodded and began to fiddle with a huge padlock.

"We'll have to break open the cage," he said at last. "Just watch that it doesn't bite; we may frighten it badly." He got out his knife and began to prise away the netting while the baby gorilla, quieter now, stared at him without expression. But Malu had not got very far with his task when a voice rang out:

"Stand away!"

Tim turned round slowly, his heart racing.

"I said – stand away."

The man with the beard was half in and half out of what appeared to be a hole in the ground.

The gun was levelled at them. The man's face was thin and bearded and his eyes blazed with anger.

"Put your gun down – and the knives."

"Do as he says," said Malu. He looked terrified and Tim, whose whole body was trembling, suddenly realised how young Malu was. Holding the gun, the man climbed out of the hole, and Tim saw that it was a kind of pit over which a wooden slat had been pulled that had scrubby, sandy grass on top. The pit was quite wide and in it was a canoe. In a flash he realised that this was Tanner's hide, but he wasn't watching nature – he had no interest in it apart from the money it could provide him with.

"OK." Tanner laughed. It was an easy-going, intimate kind of laugh, as if they were sharing an enjoyable joke, but looking at his face they all knew there was no point of contact between them whatsoever. "Now stay where you are." He was standing up now and they could see that he was tall and thin and that his clothes were stained and torn.

"You're vile," said Flower vindictively. "How can you keep that poor little creature in the cage?" She didn't seem in the least afraid and Tanner laughed again as if she had said something witty.

"He's bait," he said, confirming their fears. "I only put him in the cage yesterday."

"How long have you had him?" asked Tim angrily.

"I took him a while back, but I didn't put him out till now – I wasn't ready."

"What are you going to do?" Flower asked woodenly.

"I shall use him as a bait – I've just told you. Don't you listen? When the others come, I'll shoot them one by one." His hand shook on the barrel of his gun and Malu looked at him levelly.

Had Tanner been drinking, wondered Tim, or was he just exhausted, at the end of his stamina?

"I've been away. I thought I'd let the patrols cool down – get careless again," said Tanner. "I've been down to the south, scraping a living. Then I came back – to make some *real* money. I reckon I shall need a couple of months' trapping, organising the poachers. Then I'll have financed myself to lead a decent life somewhere else – maybe in South Africa."

"Did you take Alison Best?" asked Malu quietly.

"I employed some men to do so. I also have her husband," he added casually. "I wanted to teach them a lesson – a permanent one. They won't be in any state to protect the gorillas when I've finished with them."

Malu stared at Tanner in anguish and all three members of Green Watch exchanged horrified glances. This was a real blow. It had never occurred to them that John might be kidnapped as well.

"You realise kidnapping's a serious charge?" said Brian aggressively.

Tanner gave him one of his glittering smiles. "I've got a job to do."

"They shot my father," accused Malu, "and Mrs Best. You're responsible for that. My father could die." He broke off abruptly.

A terrible chill spread throughout Tim's whole

body. He may be obsessed, he thought, but he means every word of it – every single word.

Malu spoke quietly. "No one's above the law, and you'll get a life sentence. Let us go now, and the Bests, and give yourself up. It'll go easier for you then."

Tanner was laughing uproariously again. Obviously enjoying what to him was another really good joke, but Tim saw something in Flower's eyes that worried him even more. What was she going to do? All at once he saw her fall forwards as if she had fainted. It was very convincing, but was it convincing enough for Tanner?

He looked down at her in surprise. "Get up."

Flower gave a little moan.

"I said – get up."

She gave another moan.

"Get up!"

"She had malaria," said Malu. "She's over the worst, but —"

"Pick her up."

Slowly Malu walked towards her.

"Hurry."

He picked her up, dropped her and dived at Tanner, knocking his gun askew, grabbing his legs and pulling him down. But Tanner was wiry and strong and he was soon kicking Malu away from him. In seconds Brian and Tim were on top of him, trying to wrest the gun away, followed by Flower, making a miraculous recovery. But even the weight of all four of them wasn't enough. Tanner seemed to have an incredible strength and he threw them off within seconds. When Tim picked himself up, he saw Malu and Brian lying winded on the ground. He and Flower seemed to have remained comparatively unscathed.

"Run!" gasped Malu. He picked up a stone and threw it with unerring accuracy at Tanner, despite the obvious pain he was in. "Run – now!" The stone hit Tanner on the forehead and he staggered forward. "If you want to help us get away. Now!"

"The river," said Flower. "He'll get us on the hill. Get us easily."

A picture of the falls came into Tim's mind. How far was it? But he didn't stop to think. He followed Flower, running and diving into the river while Tanner, bleeding from the head, aimed his rifle.

"Dive!" she yelled. "Now!"

They dived under the muddy brown water, and as he did so Tim felt the current seize him.

Shots cracked out as they surfaced, but the river was wide and the current strong. In minutes Tanner's shots were falling behind them.

"Keep going," gasped Flower. "We've got to get out of range."

"We *are* out of range."

"He'll be running along the bank," she spluttered.

"He's got the others – to look after." Tim swallowed water. There was no need to make any effort at swimming – the river was taking them away from the log cabin at a faster and faster pace.

"The falls," gasped Tim eventually.

"Make for the shore."

"I can't!" yelled Tim.

"Try."

"No way."

Flower floundered past him, trying to reach the bank, but she was soon pushed back into the flow of the river. Then he saw her eyes – she was numb with horror and he suddenly remembered how terrified of the water she had always been. Their plight was bad enough but for her it must be almost impossible to keep going.

"We'll have to grab something."

"What?" yelled Tim.

The current was even stronger now and the muddy brown water had a lethal thrust to it.

"There's a log of – wood. Look!" she gasped.

"Not big enough."

"There's a bit of a tree."

"Can't reach."

"Try for that one."

"No –" He tried to grab it, missed and took in some water. He began to choke. Meanwhile the current became even faster. Was that a distant roaring he could hear?

Then Flower gasped out, "I can hear it."

"What?" But he knew – he knew.

"The falls!"

"We've had it." He'd rather drown now than go

over that dreadful height, tumbling, falling, landing
on rock if they survived that far.

"Hang on!" she shouted.

"What to?" Tim laughed hysterically and swallowed more brown, muddy water.

"There's a big tree – swim for it."

He saw what she meant: it was enormous, with
roots, scudding along at the side of the river.

"Go for it." She was desperate.

"I can't."

"Tim – you must."

"No."

"It's our only chance."

He struck out, getting in front of Flower, swimming
with fast, desperate strokes. He grabbed at a branch,
missed and fell behind, struck out again, grabbed –
and managed to make contact.

"Come on!"

"I'm coming." Flower was head down in a powerful crawl; gradually she managed to come abreast of
him and Tim was able to catch hold of her arm. She
dragged herself over him somehow, kicking and
bashing him as she went until she was in the thick of
the enormous tree roots.

"Grab me," she panted. "And pull yourself
forward."

Slowly, painfully, Tim did as he was told.

"We'll still go over," said Tim miserably, as the
tree continued to rip along at a slapping pace.

"There's a bend," replied Flower frantically.

"Can't we steer it in?" As she spoke she realised the madness of what she was saying.

"This?"

"Maybe it'll jam."

"It's got to," prayed Tim. "It's just got to."

The tree and its two passengers rounded the corner of the river at considerable speed and began to swing round.

"It's not going to jam!" yelled Tim. "It's going straight over."

Flower shouted back, "No – it's going to stick!"

"It's not!"

"It is!"

It didn't and swung back into the stream, but suddenly the undertow caught at it and forced the tree back into the bank where it finally lodged firmly.

"Come on – before it gets pushed out again," insisted Flower.

"I can't."

"Climb over."

"I can't get up."

"You've *got* to, Tim! I can feel it moving!"

Knowing this was his only chance of survival, Tim dragged himself up, fell back into the torrent and pulled himself up again. Flower was already there, standing up on the tangled roots, and with surprising strength she hauled him up the sodden wood.

"Now move – it's coming adrift."

It was; the current was gradually pushing the tree from the bank. With all his strength, Tim forced himself along behind Flower. She made the bank as, with a rending, sucking sound, the tree came away, leaving a foaming gap.

"Jump!" she roared.

He froze.

"Jump!"

And Tim took off, landing at her feet in a flurry of sodden curses.

"You made it!" she shrieked.

"I made it?"

"You did!"

"I don't believe it!"

"Look at the tree!"

They both turned to watch foliage, branches and roots sucked away from the bank and pushed into mid-stream where the current was even faster; in no time it whipped round the next bend. The roaring of the falls seemed even louder from the bank.

"Let's watch it go," she said.

"Wait —"

"Come *on*!"

She seemed to have no other desire or thought than to watch the awful death from which they had just escaped. Soaked, stumbling, they rounded the bend and watched the mighty roll of the water as it went over the falls in a majestic roar of spray. The tree surged, upended and crashed over.

"That could have been us," Flower sobbed.

"It would have been if it hadn't been for you," shouted Tim. He flung his arm round her and they did an ecstatic war dance before they fell to the sandy soil in a watery heap. Then they rolled apart, gasping, shouting, celebrating. After a while they rolled back on to their stomachs and were quiet, watching the mighty sweep of the river as it made its final death plunge downwards.

Tim looked at his watch which, amazingly, was still working. What a good advert for the makers! he thought dazedly. He must write them a letter when he got back – if he ever did get back.

"Tim," said Flower impatiently, breaking into his shocked reverie, "I said what's the time?"

"Five."

"What are we going to do?" Flower suddenly lay back, completely exhausted.

"We've got to get them out."

"How? He's terribly strong – really dangerous."

"Do you think Alison and John were in that hut?" asked Tim.

"It certainly didn't look like it," she replied.

Tim nodded. "I agree. So he must be keeping them somewhere else."

"But where? And why should he? Wouldn't it be more sensible to keep them near him?"

"Maybe. But suppose he had some help?"

"The poachers? They'd come from the villages."

"We'll have to go back and search the area thoroughly. Anyway, we can't just leave Malu and Brian," said Tim. "He won't expect us to go back again," he added shrewdly.

"We could try." She sounded doubtful. "But we

must be careful; if he catches us there'll be no chance of rescue."

"OK. We'll go up over the hill – where we were with Malu."

"Tanner's probably an expert tracker." Flower's voice was thin.

"Come on, Flower, we've got to try."

"I know," she agreed miserably.

"Unless you've got any other ideas of course," Tim said reasonably.

"No."

"Then let's go."

"I'm sorry, Tim." She stood up. "I know I'm being feeble."

"*Feeble*? You? That's impossible. You saved my life and I know how scared of the water you are. You're just exhausted and shocked – that's all."

She nodded. "I'm coming." Her voice ended in a half sob. "It's just been such a terrible day."

Tim laughed. "You're right there – a giant waterfall and Tanner."

She grinned suddenly. "It's better than being back at school anyway," she said. "Isn't it?"

"I think so," replied Tim. School would be rather calmer, he thought.

Chapter Eleven

They peered quickly through the window of the log cabin for the second time that day, taking it in turns to keep a sharp lookout for Tanner. It seemed to be completely deserted.

"What has he *done* to them?" said Flower in anguish.

"Taken them somewhere else?" Tim hazarded.

"Where?"

"Upstream. We've barely got another hour of daylight. We must get going."

"Where're we going to sleep?"

"Bivouac. But let's see what's up-river first."

"And if there's nothing?" she asked flatly.

"Then we'll have to think again."

They walked on, their fatigue telling. Suddenly Flower paused and listened carefully. "I can hear hooting," she said.

"Angus?"

"Could be any of them. Only Malu can tell the difference. Maybe they're all together, keeping pace with us somewhere in the bush. Or more likely they're making for that baby gorilla. I'm surprised we didn't find them at the hut."

"Perhaps they sense danger," said Tim, "or they're biding their time."

"Maybe that baby gorilla warned them off."

"How could it do that?" asked Tim, puzzled.

"They could have got closer – heard it warning them."

"Yes." He shivered. "It's getting cold now the sun's gone down. I'm still not used to the way the light goes just like that, without any warning."

"We'll have to make a good bivouac," she said as cheerfully as she could.

To Tim, it sounded a miserable prospect. "Pity we can't light a fire," he said bleakly.

"That would certainly give us away." She tried to laugh but failed miserably. "Hang on."

"What?"

"Down there. You can just make it out." She pointed to something beside the river – low and broken-looking. "It's a building – or was a building. See? It looks like a church."

"Perhaps it's an old mission."

"Wait – there's a light."

"Do you think —"

"We've found it? Maybe."

There was more hooting behind them and Tim found the sound immensely comforting. "What are we going to do?" he said. "We don't want to run into any more traps."

"We won't," said Flower, sounding much more purposeful than she had for some time. "We've got the darkness as cover – let's use it."

"We don't want to split up," insisted Tim fearfully.

"No need. We'll creep up together like we did at the hut."

Slowly, they advanced on the old mission. It consisted of a bell-tower, the ruined nave of a small church and a building, which might once have been living accommodation, tacked on. A small light – probably an oil lamp – shone in one of the tightly curtained windows.

"Get down," said Flower. "Right down."

They slunk in, as far below sight-level as possible, tried and failed to peer in at the lighted window and finally arrived by the bell-tower. Close up, they could see that most of it was badly ruined except for a first-floor area which was approached by an iron ladder. There was no light of any kind up there and only a half-door that looked bolted.

"I'll go up," said Tim. "I'm smaller – won't be seen against the skyline so easily."

"There isn't a skyline," replied Flower crossly, but she let him go. Suddenly she seemed to want to assert her authority, he thought. Maybe she felt her exhaustion was a sign of weakness. Tim ran lightly up the ladder and found that the door was bolted. He put his ear to the wooden panels and listened intently. He thought he could hear breathing, but perhaps it was his imagination. He just couldn't be sure. He came down again and told her.

"I suppose they must feed them – if they *are* up there," she said. "We'll have to hide somewhere and watch and wait."

It was already growing bitterly cold and they were shivering. They could hear voices from the bunkhouse now and knew they must find somewhere to shelter quickly. Looking around desperately Tim saw a pile of wood.

"Behind there?" he asked.

She looked doubtful. "Risky."

"If we go up the hill again we'll never be able to see."

"See what?" she snapped.

"Anyone—" He hesitated. "Well, anyone," he repeated.

"And what can we do if we *do* see someone?" she asked sarcastically.

Tim hadn't a clue. "We'll just have to play it by ear," he said, adding defensively, "Well, at least we'd know if someone's up there."

"We'll freeze. We can't make a bivouac down here."

"Any better ideas?"

She paused to consider. "Nothing I can think of," she said at last, with her usual candid honesty.

They went into hiding gloomily, each secretly wondering whether they were going to sit behind the woodpile all night. Minutes seemed like hours as they grew colder and colder. Once they heard a low hooting but nothing happened. Then it came again and to their intense astonishment they saw a bulky shadow moving by the side of the river. It disappeared, shortly to be replaced by another slightly smaller one. It was impossible to recognise any of them in the dark, but one thing was certain – they were gorillas. Gorillas on the prowl. But they didn't reappear and time dragged by again.

"How long have we been waiting?" demanded Flower suddenly.

"Half an hour."

"Can't have been."

"Want to borrow my watch?"

They waited again, beyond shivering now.

"Wasn't that Angus?" asked Tim.

"Where?"

"In the shadows."

"You're seeing things."

More time passed. Then a latch clicked and Flower's cold hand was on Tim's arm. "Someone's coming."

A dark figure was emerging with a tray. It was only when he began to climb the ladder that they saw he was white and familiar.

"It's him," said Flower. She sounded aghast.

"Who?"

"Him. John."

"John Best?"

"Of course it is," she hissed. "Look at him."

"Blimey!"

It was – it very definitely was. Now he was unlocking the door in the bell-tower.

"I don't get it."

"Maybe he's changed sides," whispered Flower.

"Kidnapped his own wife?"

"It's possible."

"Is it?"

"Maybe it's all a set-up," she hissed mysteriously.

"What kind of set-up?"

"I don't know. Money or something."

John went inside with the tray and quickly came out again. As he began to climb down the ladder, he paused. A shadow loomed up by the river.

"Angus!" he breathed aloud.

"I'm going to speak to him," said Tim.

"No."

"Yes – we'll freeze if I don't."

"It's too much of a risk."

"A risk we'll have to take." Without debating with her any more Tim hissed, "John!"

John whipped round.

"Over here."

He peered down.

"Here!"

John Best nodded and made his way over to them. "What are you two doing here?" he said sharply.

"What are *you* doing?" asked Flower.

"I haven't got much time." He stared over at the

lighted window. "There're only two of them at the moment."

"What are they doing letting you out?"

"Feeding Alison."

"Is she OK?" demanded Flower.

"Yes – she's in pain with her arm, but it was a clean wound."

"Are they Tanner's men?" asked Tim.

"So you know about him? Yes, they are."

"I still don't see why they allow you out like this," whispered Flower suspiciously.

"They're fed up with arguing with me about not seeing her," he said with a fleeting grin. "Anyway, they know I'd never leave her here. Tanner's really dangerous."

"But suppose you released her?"

"There's a guard up there with her. She's an African woman – one of the poacher's wives." He looked round. "I saw Angus. Is that possible?"

"They're all here," said Tim. "At least we think they are."

"The baby gorilla Tanner caught could be attracting them. I reckon it must be Sylvia's other one. The one that disappeared."

"So they'll all be here?"

"Very likely. Look, I can't be much longer —" He glanced anxiously at the lighted window. "You'd better go back and fetch —"

"How many of them in there?" asked Flower urgently.

"Two of them. But —"

"There's no time to argue," snapped Flower. "We're not going anywhere. There's no time for that."

John looked at her calmly. "You know the dangers?"

"Yes."

"Tim?"

"Of course."

"And you know they're armed?"

"Let's try it," she said firmly. "Is Tanner around?"

He looked at his watch. "He usually comes down here about eight. We've got an hour."

"What shall we do?" asked Tim.

"Give it a few minutes, and then make a racket out here."

"Will Tanner hear?" asked Tim fearfully.

"He should be too far away – so with a bit of luck, no."

"So we make a racket," whispered Flower. "What then?"

"Hopefully at least one of them will come out. Don't try to tackle him – they're both far too strong for you."

"So what *can* we do?" asked Flower.

"Keep running – and out of range. But it's dodgy—"

"We're going ahead for sure," Flower cut in. "Tanner's got Malu and Brian. We've *got* to try something."

John nodded. "Well, if you think—"

"Go back inside," said Flower urgently.

"Be careful!"

"We'll try," said Tim, looking ill. "We'll try."

Chapter Twelve

John hurried back inside and closed the door.

"What have we taken on?" asked Tim. "What are we going to do?" He felt quite helpless and Flower suddenly reached out to take his arm, to comfort him.

"Listen, we're going to scream our heads off and run about – that's all."

"But what's John going to do?"

"Try and disarm the one he's left with – and then sort out the man outside."

"So why don't we do that?"

"Don't be thick! Come on, and when we run, keep to the hillside."

"Are we going to split up?"

"We'll have to."

She went very quiet and then suddenly let go of his

arm. Standing up, she screamed loudly, "The kid-nappers are here! Go in and arrest them!"

Tim froze and Flower whacked him across the back. "Shout!" she said.

"You idiots!" yelled Tim with sudden, desperate courage. "You don't know what's going to happen to you! You're surrounded!"

"Who by?" giggled Flower, high on the danger.

"You're completely surrounded!" Tim repeated loudly. "You don't stand a chance!"

The door whipped open and a man stood in the entrance. He was holding a gun.

"Go and arrest them!" yelled Flower.

"You're surrounded!" screamed Tim.

Suddenly he realised how mistaken they had been, for surely the man would simply run back inside and barricade himself in with John and his colleague? Or would he just think they were kids and not worth worrying about? The man hesitated.

"They're just kids," he yelled to his friend inside. "Kids running about."

"What?" came from inside.

"Kids. I know who they are – that Green Watch bunch – the kids who were with Mrs Best in the land-rover."

"Them!"

"I'm going after them."

"Run!" said Flower to Tim. "And keep running."

Tim started up the hillside, his breath already coming

in great gasps out of sheer terror. Flower was running somewhere to the left of him and the man with the gun was following with easy strides. She was fast but he seemed even faster, as if running was the most natural thing in the world to him. Slowly he began to gain on her.

"Oi!" yelled Tim, acting on instinct. "Want – this – photo –" he gasped out.

The man paused and then shook his head impatiently, guessing that Tim was playing tricks with him.

"Here," panted Tim. "Come and get it." He waved his plane ticket that he had just found in the pocket of his jeans, hoping it looked sufficiently anonymous in the wan moonlight. The man changed his direction abruptly and began to pound over the grass towards Tim, who took off into the darkness as fast as he could.

Suddenly a shot rang out from below and the man stopped in his tracks as did Tim and Flower. All three of them looked down towards the door of the bunkhouse where they could just make out a shadowy figure holding a gun. Tim realised that he certainly couldn't see who it was and guessed Flower couldn't either. Could it be the other poacher? he wondered. If so, their plan had failed. Then his pursuer turned away from them and began to run back towards the mission.

Tim ran straight across to Flower. She was shaking uncontrollably.

"I thought he was going to catch me."

"He almost did."

"Who *is* it down there?" she sobbed. "John or the poacher?"

"We'll soon find out."

The shot cracked out and their pursuer fell.

"It's John."

"He shot him!" she stormed, with sudden anger.

"What else could he do? Come on!"

They ran down the hill again, and as they came near John said quietly from the shadows, "It's all right."

"Have you killed them?" asked Tim.

"No, they've both got a bullet in the leg."

Tim turned and saw that there was a man lying on the grass groaning a few metres away, while their pursuer was lying further up the hillside doing much the same.

"Won't they bleed to death?" asked Flower.

"Not if I bandage them now." He went inside, leaving Tim and Flower to stare helplessly down at the two wounded men. Quickly John Best emerged with a first aid kit and a spray canister. "This won't take long," he said and stood over the poacher he had shot first. "Try to relax," he said gently. "I'm going to apply a pain relief spray; the bullet only gave you a flesh wound but you won't like walking on it."

"It's in my leg!" gasped the poacher.

"Rubbish!" said John as he bent down over the wounded man. Then he glanced further up the hillside. "The same will apply to you. There are no bullets in either of your legs – I'll guarantee you."

"How can you be sure?" demanded Flower. "You were firing in the dark and—"

"I've had to put wounded animals out of their misery," said John, "so I've become a bit of a crack shot. Want to take a look?"

She shook her head and John looked at his watch.

"We've got to hurry – Tanner will be on his way."

He moved on to the next man.

"Wait," said Flower. "That woman – the one who's with Alison – why hasn't she heard anything?"

"Because she is a heavy sleeper, I should think. She'd sleep through anything, that one." He tied the bandage gently while the man swore viciously at him. "OK," he stood up. "Let's get to her." He paused. "No Tanner yet – not that we can see." His voice shook.

"You mean – he could be watching for us?" asked Tim.

John ignored him and ran up the ladder, opened the door with the key he'd taken from the bunkhouse and pushed the gun into the entrance.

"Get up!"

There was a sleepy groan and Alison said, "You're forgetting something."

"What?"

"I'm handcuffed to her."

"Damn!"

There was another sleepy groan and a deep voice said, "Just what's going on?"

"I have your husband here," said John crisply.

"I've already wounded him. If you don't unlock those handcuffs I'll kill him!"

"You're lying."

"Want to take a look?"

"You're lying," the woman repeated.

"OK." John turned and yelled down to the nearest poacher. "Tell her!" But he said nothing.

"Tell her!" said Flower, gazing around frantically.

Tim felt sick; Tanner could be waiting there now, about to shoot everyone. They could have seconds to live. "Tell her!" he snarled, kicking out at the man. "Tell her!"

The poacher paused, looking up.

"I mean it," said John, turning the gun on him.

"You're bluffing," the man said, grinning, but his voice lacked conviction.

John fired twice and the bullets hit the ground just above his head. The grin turned to a look of terror.

"Don't shoot me!"

"Then tell her."

"He means it, Somi – he means it. *Do* something."

"I don't have the key."

"Yes you do!" he yelled. "It's in your pocket. Now, unlock those handcuffs."

Slowly she did as she was told and Alison came stiffly out. Her shoulder was bandaged and she looked pale and strained.

"Hallo, you two," she said. "How did—"

"We haven't got time!" snapped John. "Come down. And you, Somi – you stay up there. I *said* stay up there – unless you want the shooting to start again." The woman's head disappeared.

Just then more shots cracked out further up the valley, followed by a howl of animal pain.

"Angus?" said Flower.

"Albert?" Tim wheeled round on John Best.

"That's why he hasn't come," he muttered.

"What do you mean?" yelled Tim.

"I think he's caught the gorillas trying to get at the cage – to release his prisoner."

"You mean they'd try to break it down?" asked Flower wonderingly.

"Well. I've seen them get their own kind out of traps, so why not out of a cage?"

"But now—"

"I'll get up there," said John. "Fast."

Alison had said nothing, but when she did speak, she voiced everyone's fears. "He's shot one of them."

There was a total silence, then John repeated, "I must go – get up there."

"We'll both go," said Alison. "You kids stay here – keep an eye on—"

"No," said Flower.

"Not a chance," returned Tim.

John Best shrugged. "It's no good," he said. "You can't keep these two out of the action."

Unwillingly Alison gave in.

"Keep on up the hill," said John.

By now they were getting used to climbing and then looking down on danger. They were nearing Tanner's hut when Alison suddenly paused. She was staring at the point where the treeline finished at the top of the hill.

Tim saw the dark shapes at once. There must have been about twenty of them – maybe more – standing sentinel-like, looking down on the hut and the river.

"Isn't that Angus?" said Flower. "That very big one?"

Alison nodded. "That's him. Group Two must have joined up with another group. There're so many of them."

"What are we going to do?"

"Check on Malu and Brian – what else?"

"But is he all right?" asked Tim. "Is Angus all right?"

"No," said John quickly. "Look at the way he is."

Then Tim saw that Angus was half standing, half leaning against the dead trunk of an old tree, making tiny grunting noises. Another gorilla, a strange female, suddenly took his head and began to stroke it.

"We've got to help him," said Flower desperately.

"We've got to help your brother and Malu first," said John decisively.

"Where on earth is Tanner?" muttered Tim as they slowly and cautiously approached the hut. Lights blazed from its windows and the front door was half open.

"It's a trap," said Flower.

"I'm not so sure." Alison stared hard at the silent building. "Maybe he's taken to the river."

Tim could just make out the cage. It was badly damaged but the baby gorilla was still inside. So Angus hadn't succeeded in his rescue plan. Was that why the gorillas were still hovering?

"I'm going over there," said Alison. "And I expect everyone to stay where they are, particularly you two," she added, glancing fiercely at Flower and Tim. Without saying anything, John passed her one of the guns and she moved slowly forward, looking to right and to left.

"It's a trap," whispered Flower again.

Neither John nor Tim made any comment as they watched her arrive at the open door of the lighted cabin.

Alison was inside for what seemed a very long time. When she came out she beckoned them over.

"Where are they?" asked John as he joined her.

"The gorillas must have got inside; either that or there's been a terrible fight. The place is wrecked. And empty. You'd better come over and take a look."

She was right. The interior of the cabin was totally devastated and there was hardly a piece of furniture that remained undamaged. Then Flower noticed a long, fresh stain down one wall.

"What is it?" she asked. But she knew.

"Nothing," replied John weakly.

"It's blood," replied Alison quietly.

"Human?" Tim whispered.

"I don't know." Alison seemed almost impatient. "Where could they all have got to?"

"Brian – Malu," rapped Flower. "We've got to find them." Then she had a sudden thought. "They're in the hole – maybe – in his hideous hole."

She took them out to the back and, with Alison pointing the rifle down at the hatch, slid it back. They were there, bound hand and foot but unharmed. Tim cried out in glorious relief.

Once John had untied their bonds, Brian and Malu struggled stiffly out of their coffin-like prison.

"What happened?" asked Flower.

"He was awful," said Brian in a choked voice.

"He was furious – said we were interfering with his livelihood," put in Malu. "Kept insisting he'd have to kill us like he was going to kill every gorilla in the park. He seems to really hate them now. Then we heard some shots further up—"

"That was us," said John.

For the first time Brian and Malu saw Alison standing in the darkness.

"Thank God!" Tears poured down Malu's face while Brian kept saying over and over again, "It's like some kind of miracle."

"Where is he?" asked Alison warily.

"He put us in that terrible hole," said Malu. "I think he was beginning to panic. Didn't really know what to do. Then we heard the gorillas. They tried to break open the cage and went into the cabin. They must have smashed everything; there was an amazing amount of breaking and roaring. Then there was a shot and they all disappeared."

"Tanner must have gone too."

"I hope so." Brian looked around him, as if the nightmare was about to start all over again.

"Perhaps he heard the shots and went to see what was happening further up the river," Malu suggested. "What *was* happening?"

"We haven't got time to talk," said John, and as he spoke another shot cracked out followed by an answering squeal of animal pain.

Alison was pale and grimly determined. "It must be Tanner," she said. "We've got to stop him."

"Come on," said Flower. "Now!"

"He's probably got plenty of ammunition." John checked the breach of his own rifle. "And I've only got four bullets left."

Another shot and another and then another. But there was no response – no answering cries of pain.

"Come *on*!" Flower was beside herself.

"I'll check the cabin for more ammunition—"

"No," she said. "Please come now!"

"Shut up," John said brusquely and darted back into the cabin.

"I know," said Alison, putting her arm round

Flower's heaving shoulders. "But we've got to be ready."

After what seemed agonising hours, John came out.

"Nothing," he said. "I can't find anything – in all that mess."

"Let's go," said Tim.

"He's probably heavily armed and dangerous," said John sharply. "This isn't a cops and robbers film."

Flower gazed at him angrily. "Who says it is?" she asked.

They set off up the hill yet again, keeping together as a group behind Malu, who had naturally taken the lead.

"He went this way," he said, looking down at tracks only he could see. "To the side here. Keep by the bushes, and if I say get down, dive on your faces."

They carried on, expecting something to happen any moment. To Tim, George Tanner seemed to lurk behind every bush and every tree. Looking up, he could no longer see the gorillas. Angus must have been helped away because there was no sign of his enormous bulk – nor of any other wounded gorillas.

Then, very abruptly, they heard the pulsating, pounding sound, which died away as quickly as it had started. It began again, and with it a chorus of powerful barking.

"What's happening?" Brian asked.

Malu turned back, his hand raised for them to stop. "They're beating their chests," he said.

"What does that mean?" asked Flower fearfully.

"It usually means they're angry and afraid," said Alison. "And there seem to be a lot more than just Group Two."

"They must have been joined by a group from this side of the waterfall – ones we don't know at all," said Malu.

As he spoke, a cry rang out, and for a moment Tim couldn't work out whether it was animal or human.

"I think they've got George Tanner," said John Best suddenly. "God help him!"

"Go on, Malu," said Alison. "Just keep going."

"But they'll be—"

"We have to do what we can to help him," she said.

"Why?"

"Because he's a human being," she snapped.

Malu hurried on and then broke into a run. Behind him, they all started to dart towards the sound of a second appalling scream.

They were gathered together in a dark glade which the moonlight barely penetrated. The gorillas were sitting on their haunches or on all fours and Tim recognised Sylvia and her baby Tommy but none of the others. George Tanner was lying in the centre of the circle of dark, powerful forms. His face was covered with blood and his rifle was lying smashed to one side. Tanner's face twisted round to them, and Tim had never seen such stark terror in a person's eyes before.

"Help me," he whispered. "You've got to help me."

But as they approached, the male gorillas rose to their feet and began to pound their chests again. The noise was the most frightening Tim had ever heard, and when he looked across at Flower and Brian he could see that they were as petrified as he was. Malu looked very worried and only John and Alison seemed calm, almost confident.

"Shut up!" said Alison.

"You've got—" Tanner practically gibbered at them.

"I said – shut up or they'll kill you. Lie still." She walked straight into the glade, and then sat down in front of Tanner, making a chuckling, hooting sound. The male gorillas stared down at her, until one of them that Tim now recognised as Albert walked slowly towards her. He could see that the fur on his leg was matted with blood. Alison moved slowly towards him and then stroked his wound. Albert sat down beside her and made his "huh-huh" sound. Leaving him she walked slowly towards Angus, whose chest and shoulder were also covered in blood, some of which looked bright and freshly flowing. Again, she stroked the wound, gently, carefully making the same soft "huh-huh" sound. There was a great silence amongst the gorillas. At last she moved

131

slowly towards Tanner and sat down beside him. Again making the sound, she began to stroke his bloodied face.

It's a miracle, thought Tim, and then he wasn't so sure. There was a strange mystical logic to it – one that the gorillas seemed to accept naturally. Soon she got up and went back to Angus, crouching in front of him while Tanner breathed: "Don't leave me – please don't leave me."

But Alison completely ignored him. She continued to crouch in front of Angus, who looked down at her with a kind of weary humility. Then she walked back to Tanner. "Do exactly what I say or they'll kill us all." Her voice was very low and even.

"Don't—"

"Just do what I say. Stand up slowly. Very slowly.

He did as he was told, staggering slightly as he got to his feet.

"Do *everything* slowly. Turn and walk out of the glade – and down the hill, back to the cabin."

"What am I going to do there?"

"I'll tell you. Shut up and keep moving." Her voice was soft but steely. As she passed the others, Alison said, "Angus will be coming – I hope." The other gorillas crouched, staring at them, and Tim hoped very sincerely that Brian's eyes wouldn't be drawn to any of them. "Follow me," she said.

Yes, thought Tim. It's OK. He's keeping his eyes down. Slowly the human procession walked out of the glade. Hesitantly, Angus followed.

They walked in single file down the hillside in the moonlight: Tanner, Alison with the rifle that John had just handed to her, John himself, Flower, Brian, Tim, Malu – and Angus, some metres behind them but definitely following. It was the strangest moment of Tim's whole life.

"What now?" asked Tanner.

"You open that cage."

"And let the monkey go?" His voice was a little more confident now and a trace of arrogance and hatred was beginning to emerge.

"Let the gorilla go," she said.

"And then?"

"We'll take you in; you've broken plenty of laws to do with the gorillas, and as far as the humans are concerned we can start with kidnapping and attempted murder."

"Sentimental fools!" he sneered. "We were all doing nicely until you interfered."

"Except the gorillas," Alison pointed out quietly. "Now, open that cage."

"I've got no key."

She prodded him in the back with the rifle. "Get it."

"I don't—"

"Get it!"

With sudden decision, Tanner felt in his back pocket and reluctantly produced the key.

"Open the cage."

With equal reluctance he opened it.

"And stand back."

133

Alison passed John the rifle and he covered Tanner while she knelt down by the open door of the cage and began to make the now familiar "huh-huh" sound again. Tim watched the baby gorilla come slowly out of the cage. Then he heard the hooting and turned to see the guardian, Angus, standing a few metres up the hillside, calling. The baby gorilla hesitated and then ran up towards Angus, who clasped him in his arms. Then he turned and began to limp slowly away, his precious burden held close to his massive, wounded chest.

While John and Malu tied Tanner's hands, the three members of Green Watch could hardly trust themselves to speak. Then Flower chokingly asked Alison, "Will Angus survive?"

"Yes, I think he will."

"Can't you help him?"

"Yes. If Group Two come back to the base camp – as I'm sure they will – John can use one of his tranquilliser darts and dress his wound for him."

"Will he give the baby back to Sylvia?" asked Brian.

"Yes, you can be sure of that," replied Alison gently.

They watched Angus slowly limping into the trees, the baby gorilla clasped to him. Then he disappeared from view.

MYSTERY THRILLER

Introducing, a new series of hard hitting, action packed thrillers for young adults.

THE SONG OF THE DEAD by Anthony Masters
For the first time in years 'the song of the dead' is heard around the mud flats of Whitstable. But this time is it really the ghostly cries of dead sailors? Or is it something far more sinister? Barney Hampton is sure that something strange is going on – and he's determined to get to the bottom of the mystery . . .

THE FERRYMAN'S SON by Ian Strachan
Rob is convinced that Drewe and Miles are up to no good. Why else would two sleek city whizz-kids want to spend the summer yachting around a sleepy Devonshire village? Where do they go on their frequent night cruises? And why does the lovely Kimberley go with them? Then Kimberley disappears, and Rob finds himself embroiled in a web of deadly intrigue . . .

Further titles to look out for in the Mystery Thriller series:

Treasure of Grey Manor by Terry Deary
The Foggiest by Dave Belbin
Blue Murder by Jay Kelso
Dead Man's Secret by Linda Allen
Crossfire by Peter Beere
The Third Dragon by Garry Kilworth
Vanishing Point by Anthony Masters

THE BABYSITTERS CLUB

Need a babysitter? Then call the Babysitters Club. Kristy Thomas and her friends are all experienced sitters. They can tackle any job from rampaging toddlers to a pandemonium of pets. To find out all about them, read on!

Look out for:

The Babysitters Club No 15:
Little Miss Stoneybrook . . . and Dawn £1.75
The Babysitters Club No 16:
Jessi's Secret Language £1.75
The Babysitters Club No 17:
Mary Anne's Bad Luck Mystery £1.75
The Babysitters Club No 18:
Stacey's Mistake £1.75
The Babysitters Club No 19:
Claudia and the Bad Joke £1.75
The Babysitters Club No 20:
Kristy and the Walking Disaster £1.99
The Babysitters Club No 21:
Mallory and the Trouble with Twins £1.99
The Babysitters Club No 22:
Jessi Ramsey, Pet-sitter £1.99
The Babysitters Club No 23:
Dawn on the Coast £1.99
The Babysitters Club No 24:
Kristy and the Mother's Day Surprise £1.99

You'll find these and many more fun Hippo books at your local bookseller, or you can order them direct. Just send off to Customer Services, Hippo Books, Westfield Road, Southam, Leamington Spa, Warwickshire CV33 0JH, not forgetting to enclose a cheque or postal order for the price of the book(s) plus 30p per book for postage and packing.

GREEN WATCH by Anthony Masters

GREEN WATCH is a new series of fast moving environmental thrillers, in which a group of young people battle against the odds to save the natural world from ruthless exploitation. All titles are printed on recycled paper.

BATTLE FOR THE BADGERS
Tim's been sent to stay with his weird Uncle Seb and his two kids, Flower and Brian, who run Green Watch – an environmental pressure group. At first Tim thinks they're a bunch of cranks – but soon he finds himself battling to save badgers from extermination . . .

SAD SONG OF THE WHALE
Tim leaps at the chance to join Green Watch on an anti-whaling expedition. But soon, he and the other members of Green Watch, find themselves shipwrecked and fighting for their lives . . .

DOLPHIN'S REVENGE
The members of Green Watch are convinced that Sam Jefferson is mistreating his dolphins – but how can they prove it? Not only that, but they must save Loner, a wild dolphin, from captivity . . .

MONSTERS ON THE BEACH
The Green Watch team is called to investigate a suspected radiation leak. Teddy McCormack claims to have seen mutated crabs and sea-plants, but there's no proof, and Green Watch don't know whether he's crazy or there's been a cover-up . . .

SPIRIT OF THE CONDOR

Green Watch has gone to California on a surfing holiday – but not for long! Someone is trying to kill the Californian Condor, the bird cherished by an Indian tribe – the Daiku – without which the tribe will die. Green Watch must struggle to save both the Condor and the Daiku . . .